EVIL
DECEPTION

REVISED EDITION

BRUCE S. POTEAT

Copyright © 2025 Bruce S. Poteat.

All rights reserved. No part of this book may be reproduced, stored, or transmitted by any means—whether auditory, graphic, mechanical, or electronic—without written permission of both publisher and author, except in the case of brief excerpts used in critical articles and reviews. Unauthorized reproduction of any part of this work is illegal and is punishable by law.

ISBN: 979-8-89419-695-4 (sc)
ISBN: 979-8-89419-696-1 (hc)
ISBN: 979-8-89419-697-8 (e)

Because of the dynamic nature of the Internet, any web addresses or links contained in this book may have changed since publication and may no longer be valid. The views expressed in this work are solely those of the author and do not necessarily reflect the views of the publisher, and the publisher hereby disclaims any responsibility for them.

One Galleria Blvd., Suite 1900, Metairie, LA 70001
(504) 702-6708

CONTENTS

Dedication v
Preface vii
Introduction ix

Chapter 1   Satan Tries to Kill the Seed and Thaw God's Plan 1
Chapter 2   Satan Tries to Disrupt the Crucifixion 7
Chapter 3   Week of the Passover 14
Chapter 4   The High Priest Demands Death 18
Chapter 5   Jesus' Body 32
Chapter 6   Simon of Cyrene weeks prior to the Crucifixion 34
Chapter 7   Satan Tempts Joseph and Nicodemus 40
Chapter 8   Simon Hides from the Evil One 46
Chapter 9   Alexander Follows Simon 54
Chapter 10 Joseph Bargains for Jesus' Body 57
Chapter 11 Simon's Death 65
Chapter 12 Alexander is Protected 69
Chapter 13 The Hair is Removed 72
Chapter 14 Satan Returns to the Tomb 82
Chapter 15 Alex's Journey Home 86
Chapter 16 Battle on Earth 96
Chapter 17 Alexander's Second Journey 106

Chapter 18	The Voice Confronts Dr. Spigelman	112
Chapter 19	The Professor Meets Debi from Genealogy	118
Chapter 20	The Professor Meets the Voice	121
Chapter 21	Debi calls Professor Gefen	128
Chapter 22	Alexander (the Voice) is in Danger	134
Chapter 23	The Professor is Haunted by Faceless Hoodies	137
Chapter 24	Professor Gefen Investigates	143
Chapter 25	The Voice is Revealed	151
Chapter 26	Debi Takes the Document	158
Chapter 27	Lucifer Hears the Name "Simon"	162
Chapter 28	The Document is Stolen	168
Chapter 29	War Two Thousand Years in the Future	173
Chapter 30	Debi Prays	179
Chapter 31	The Discovery: Three Months Later	181

DEDICATION

This book is a tribute to my late mother, Orene Sanders Poteat, who was my source of inspiration throughout my life. She was a woman of strong character and unwavering faith. Her earthly journey came to an end on August 24, 2012, but her legacy lives on. Through my personal encounter with Jesus, I have come to know Him as my Lord and Savior, and my mother's words only reaffirmed this truth. I am certain that I will be reunited with my dear mother and father someday.

Moreover, I extend my heartfelt dedication to Debi, my beloved wife of 36 years. Debi has bravely battled stage 4 cancer, and despite all the challenges, she never failed to support and encourage me to complete this book. Debi, I love you dearly. (Since the first release of Evil Deception Debi Passed away, November 9, 2022.)

I also want to express my gratitude to my lifelong friend, Pattie Smith, for her unwavering encouragement, and to Riley Million, a talented graphic artist who worked closely with me to design the book cover. Thank you, Pattie and Riley, for your invaluable contributions.

PREFACE

Prepare yourself for a gripping tale of deception, betrayal, and the ultimate battle between good and evil. In God's warning of the end times, He fore saw the world being misled and led astray. (Mathew24:24-25). But what if the deception was even greater than we could imagine? In Evil Deception, you will witness the cunning and calculated plans of the enemy, based on real-life events that lay the groundwork for this powerful and thought-provoking fictional story. As the plot unfolds, you will come face to face with the lies that Satan will use to bring about the downfall of the Christian religion. The apostate church will crumble, and souls will be lost forever. For Satan's goal has always been to deny Christ and all that He stands for, His existence, His miracles, and even His resurrection.

With relentless determination, Satan will stop at nothing to destroy the church and claim victory over the souls of humanity.

But this is not just a story. It is a warning, a warning of a catastrophic event that will shatter the world as we know it. It is not a natural disaster or a man-made catastrophe, but the arrival of the Antichrist. As foretold in the Bible, false prophets and deceitful leaders will rise, performing miracles and wonders to deceive even the most faithful of God's followers. Are you prepared for the ultimate test of your faith? And at the heart of this tale lies a deeper mystery. A mystery that will challenge your beliefs and make you question everything you thought you knew.

This is not a book that seeks to teach theology, but rather, to spark discussion and inspire you to think outside the box. So come, join us on this journey of discovery and revelation. Let yourself be drawn into a world of intrigue and danger, where nothing is as it seems. Through vivid descriptions and a rich narrative, Evil Deception will ignite your senses and emotions like never before. Are you ready to face the ultimate battle between good and evil? The choice is yours.

INTRODUCTION

Evil Deception is a gripping and thought-provoking book that will take you on a journey through time and space. With its unparalleled intensity, this book will push the limits of your imagination and leave you questioning everything you thought you knew about Satan's ability to deceive. Through a masterful blend of biblical events and storytelling, Evil Deception tells the tale of a young boy named Alexander who witnesses the crucifixion of Jesus and uncovers a sinister plot by Satan to deceive the world during the end times.

Alexander's bravery and determination to stop Satan's plans make him a complex and intriguing character that will capture your heart and imagination. But this is not just a story of good versus evil. It's a story that will evoke strong emotions within you as you witness the heart-wrenching sacrifices made by Alexander and the people he loves. And with the help of the archangel Michael, Alexander's journey will take you to the 21st century, where the fate of the world hangs in the balance.

With its vivid and sensory prose, Evil Deception will transport you to the very depths of Satan's cunning and deceit. Every page will leave you on the edge of your seat, eagerly turning to the next as you experience the intense battle between good and evil. So, buckle up and prepare to be swept away by this character-rich and emotionally charged tale.

Father please forgive them!

They called Me King of the Jews and placed a crown upon my head;

How quickly forgotten was the healing of the sick, and the raising of the dead;

They tied me to a post and scourged me with a whip; My Flesh ripped apart by the metal bits on the tip;

My skull was pierced by the thorns, a crown I did not own; Blood flowed across my battered face, destine to atone,

My eyes were swollen almost shut, from beatings dusk to dawn; My back was bleeding badly; my strength was long since gone,

I stumbled under the weight of all the human sins; I fell to the ground, while the crowds jeered again;

The Roman soldier kicked Me but no one offered a hand; Until a stranger came walking by and the soldier grabbed this man,

Tears ran down my cheeks as this stranger pull away; but once he looked into my eyes he knew he had to stay,

He ushered Me to my feet as we slowly got on our way; Not a word was spoken between us as we communicated that day,

Simon helped Me complete My mission one Satan fought to stay; Simon helped Me to the cross and is with Me till this day,

The rusty spikes tore through My flesh hanging Me to the cross,

The spear thrust into My side and blood and water were lost,

My life was failing fast but the worst was yet to come, for My Father's face would turn away, as sin covered His Son,

I knew this day was coming it was talked about from time past; My time on earth was short, but the prophecies were fulfilled at last,

I came not to condemn the world but to provide you with a path; a door is open to the Father from the future to the past,

My love is now completed the rest is up to you; Father please forgive them for they know not what they do.

© B. J. Poteat

CHAPTER 1

SATAN TRIES TO KILL THE SEED AND THAW GOD'S PLAN

When sin entered the world, it became a dark cloud that threatened to consume all of humanity. It was a poison that seeped into the hearts of men and women, corrupting their very souls. And in the midst of this chaos, a written document emerged, a beacon of light and hope in a world shrouded in darkness. We call this document the Bible, and it is a record of events that have shaped our past, present, and future. But this was not just any document. It was God's word, His divine instruction for His creation. Through the pages of the Bible, we see the hand of God guiding us, teaching us, and warning us. And from the very beginning, God had a plan – a plan to save us from the grip of sin and death. But Satan, the enemy of God, had other plans. Long before Adam and Eve were even created, Satan rebelled against God and declared war on Him. He wanted nothing more than to overthrow the Almighty and rule over all creation.

So, when God created Adam and placed him over all things on earth, Satan saw his opportunity. He launched a vicious and deceiving attack, targeting Adam and all of humanity. And unfortunately, he was successful. Adam gave in to temptation, and in that moment, man came under the curse of Almighty God. The sands of time were released, and the time clock of death started ticking. But God, in His infinite wisdom, had a plan. He would thwart Satan's ultimate victory and reveal a plan of redemption – a way for humanity to be saved and for Satan to be ultimately defeated. But Satan would not go down without a fight. He would continue to wage war against God and His creation.

And after he successfully tempted Adam and Eve, a declaration of war was made. God spoke to Satan and said, "And I will put enmity between thee and the woman, and between thy seed and her seed: It shall bruise thy head, and thou shalt bruise his heel." These words struck fear into Satan's heart as he realized that this was how he would be defeated. So as the battle rages on, the forces of good and evil locked in an eternal struggle. But we have hope, for we know that ultimately, good will triumph over evil. And as we wait for the final victory, we must remain vigilant, for Satan will stop at nothing to bring us down. But with God by our side, we can stand firm and fight against the darkness, knowing that in the end, we will emerge victorious. The seed of the woman was the Lord Jesus Christ Himself.

It was a promise spoken by God, a promise of a Savior who would bring redemption to the world. And with that promise came a looming threat, a threat that Satan would stop at nothing to prevent the fulfillment of this prophecy. Satan's first attempt was with Eve, the mother of all living. He whispered lies and deceit, tempting her to eat from the forbidden tree. And when she and Adam did, he thought he had won. But God had a plan, a plan that would not be thwarted by Satan's schemes. As Eve gave birth to her first two sons, Cain and Abel, Satan watched intently, waiting to see which would be the chosen one. When God accepted Abel's offering and rejected Cain's, Satan's jealousy took hold. He moved Cain to kill his own brother, hoping to end the line of the promised seed. But God had other plans, and from Eve's womb came another son, Seth.

Satan's attempts continued as the generations passed. He spread wickedness and corruption, hoping to corrupt the seed of the woman. But God preserved His chosen line, bringing forth men and women of faith, who would play crucial roles in the coming of the Messiah. And then, finally, the long-awaited Savior was born. The seed of the woman, the promised Redeemer, entered the world in the humble form of a baby. Satan's greatest fear had come to pass, and he knew that his days were numbered. But even in the face of defeat, he would not give up his relentless pursuit to destroy this Savior. With every step Jesus took, Satan was there, tempting and testing, trying to derail God's plan. And in the end, he thought he had won when it looked like Jesus' crucifixion on the cross would not take place as written. But little did he know, that was all part of God's perfect plan. For through Jesus' death and resurrection, He defeated Satan once and for all, fulfilling the promise of the seed of the woman and bringing salvation to all who believe.

Even through the face of evil and darkness, God's promise still stood strong, and the seed of the woman prevailed. And today, we can stand firm in the knowledge that no matter what battles we may face, God's promises will always triumph in the end.

Satan set out on a diabolical tactic, one that would corrupt and pervert mankind's very nature. He began a campaign of temptation, of luring humanity into a web of sin and immorality. And oh, how he succeeded. The whole human race, with the exception of Noah and his family, was consumed by sexual corruption. It seemed as though Satan's plan was foolproof, his grip on mankind unbreakable. But God had other plans. In a moment of divine intervention, God sent a massive flood to destroy Satan's work. Only Noah and his family, the faithful few, were spared. And from their lineage, God's plan of salvation would continue.

But Satan was not finished. As time went on, Satan saw an opportunity to thwart God's promise of a blessing unto Abraham's seed. Sarah, Abraham's wife, was barren. So, Satan tempted Abraham to have a child with his servant girl, Hagar, in an attempt to counterfeit God's plan. But God's plan could not be counterfeited, and Sarah miraculously gave birth to Isaac. Isaac married Rebekah, but she too was barren. Once again, Satan saw an opportunity to derail God's plan. But God intervened and Rebekah conceived. From her womb came Jacob and Esau, two brothers locked in a struggle for the birthright. Satan saw a chance to destroy the one through whom the Messiah would come.

Satan's hatred for God's chosen people intensified. He tried to destroy them in Egypt, using Pharaoh as a type of antichrist. Pharaoh ordered all male babies to be killed, hoping to wipe out the seed of Israel. But God intervened once again, raising up Moses, a child found floating in the Nile River, to lead His people out of bondage. Then, in a moment of great danger, when it seemed as though all hope was lost, God spared the royal seed of the house of Judah. One boy, Joash, was hidden in the temple for six years, shielded from Satan's deadly grasp. He was the only person on the earth through whom the Messiah could come. The weight of the world rested on his shoulders, and the forces of evil were constantly working to bring him down. But God had a plan, and he would not let Satan prevail. Though Satan's attempts were relentless, God's plan could not be thwarted.

During the time of Esther, Satan used a man named Haman to make a decree to kill all Jews young and old. The darkness of this decree hung over the land like a heavy cloud, threatening to wipe out an entire nation. But through God's everlasting plan, he would not let Satan have the final say. In the face of such overwhelming opposition, God raised up Esther and Mordecai to be his instruments of salvation. They were just ordinary people, but God used them in extraordinary ways. Through their bravery and faith, the nation was spared from destruction, and the name of God was glorified.

But Satan's attacks did not stop there. As God continued to rise up hero's within the pages of the Bible, Satan continued to target God's chosen people, with one of his greatest attempts was the story of David and Goliath. The Philistine giant stood before the armies of Israel, taunting and intimidating them with his massive size and strength. But God had a plan, and he would not let Satan's champion have the victory. David, a mere shepherd boy, stepped forward to face Goliath. He was small and unassuming, but he carried with him the power of God. With just a sling and a stone, he stood against the giant and declared, "You come against me with sword and spear and javelin, but I come against you in the name of the Lord Almighty." And in that moment, the whole world held its breath as the battle between good and evil played out before them. As David's stone struck Goliath's forehead, the earth shook, and the heavens rejoiced. The enemy was defeated, and the people could do nothing but stand in awe of the God of Israel. In that moment, it was clear that this was not just a physical battle, but a spiritual one as well. And the victory belonged to the Lord.

Through stories like these, we see the power of God at work. He used ordinary people to accomplish extraordinary things, and he showed that nothing is impossible for him. So let us never underestimate the strength and love of our God, for he is always working behind the scenes, orchestrating the greatest upsets of all times. But these are just a few of the many attempts by Satan to stop the seed of God's plan.

From the moment Jesus was born, the enemy had been relentlessly seeking to destroy him. When Herod ordered the massacre of all male babies, Satan stood ready to devour the promised Messiah. But God's divine protection was always at work. From the wise men being warned in a dream to escape, to Mary and Joseph being directed to flee to Egypt, God's hand was evident in preserving the life of His precious Son. Throughout Jesus's life, Satan continued to tempt and plot against him, trying to derail God's perfect plan. Even on the cross, he whispered lies and taunted Jesus to give up and take the easy way out.

But Satan's ultimate goal was to deceive and destroy the world. His lies and deception would lead many astray, even causing some to turn from God in the last days. But we must remember, God's plan will always prevail, and Satan's schemes will be ultimately defeated.

CHAPTER 2

SATAN TRIES TO DISRUPT THE CRUCIFIXION

The Son of God appeared on the horizon, a figure of power and authority that radiated with divine light. His very presence sent shivers down the spines of all those who dared to oppose Him. The reason for His appearance was clear: to destroy the Devil's work. With every step He took, the ground beneath Him trembled, for He was on a mission to bring down the forces of evil that had plagued humanity for far too long. As He walked, His eyes flashed with determination, His jaw set in a firm line. He was not here to play games or make idle threats. He had come to conquer and conquer He would. And so, He did, disarming the powers and authorities with ease. In a spectacular display of strength, He made a public spectacle of them, triumphing over them by the cross.

But this was not the first time the Son of God had faced off against the Devil. No, He had been locked in a battle of wills with the Prince of Darkness since the beginning of His earthly ministry. And with each confrontation, He emerged victorious. The Devil's attempts to tempt Him away from His devotion and love for God were futile, for the Son of God was unshakable in His resolve. And as He stood before the Devil, the Son of God declared, "The prince of this world will be driven out." His words echoed with power and authority, striking fear into the heart of Satan. For he knew that Jesus had a hold over him, and that with each victory, the Son of God was taking away what he held most dear—the captive world. But as the time for the Son of God's ultimate triumph drew near, Satan's desires for revenge intensified. He knew that his time was running out, and that he had to stop the seed before the cross. For if Jesus were to fulfill the prophecies and die on the cross, Satan's fate would be sealed. And so, a battle of epic proportions began, a chess match between good and evil, with the fate of humanity hanging in the balance. But with each move, the Son of God was one step ahead, his unwavering determination leading him to victory. And in the end, it was the Son of God who emerged as the ultimate victor, for He had fulfilled the prophecies and conquered the forces of darkness once and for all.

As Jesus approached the Passover week, His senses were heightened, his mind sharp with knowledge of Satan's presence. The adversary circled like a vulture, waiting for the perfect moment to strike. But Jesus, wise and deliberate, spoke openly to His disciples of the coming events - His death and resurrection. Satan grew desperate, knowing that the fate of the world hung in the balance. He could not afford to act too soon. The disciples, still naive and ignorant, could not grasp the gravity of Jesus' words. They could not fathom how He could boldly march in to Jerusalem, knowing the Sanhedrin's sentence of death. Their minds were clouded by their own expectations, their own desires for an earthly kingdom. They could not comprehend that Jesus would die at the hands of the very ones He came to save. And in this moment of doubt and confusion,

Satan saw an opportunity. He entered Peter, the future "Rock" of the church, and tempted Jesus with his words, "Don't say that, Lord. This will never happen to you." But Jesus, seeing through Peter's facade, saw Satan within him. He commanded the devil to leave and get behind Him. Both Jesus and Satan knew the importance of the upcoming events. The fate of humanity hung in the balance, and they were both aware of the pivotal role they played. And so, as the days approached, the tension grew, emotions ran high, and the battle between good and evil intensified. The outcome was set, but both sides were ready to give their all.

Satan's actions struck a devastating blow, causing Lazarus' death and bringing immense pain to Jesus. But this was just one instance of his cunning tactics. The malicious mastermind was also responsible for the death of John the Baptist, the fearless forerunner and beloved cousin of Jesus. He was waging a despicable terrorist attack on those closest to Christ, and the Son of God knew it all too well. Satan knew Jesus cherished Lazarus deeply, and he used this as a twisted calling card to taunt and torment Him. His expertise in psychological warfare was evident as he attempted to weaken and distract Jesus from His divine mission, luring Him back to the dangerous territory of Judea where the high priests were plotting His death thus foregoing the cross.

It was a diabolical message, sending a chilling warning that even family and friends were not safe if Christ was not there to protect them. Jesus wept for the loss of John and Lazarus; He also felt the heavy weight of Satan's schemes. But in a moment of divine power and authority, He called out to Lazarus with an unparalleled miracle: "Lazarus, come forth." With these words, Jesus proved that His word and authority were not mere empty promises, but were truly "living and powerful, and sharper than any two-edged sword." And in turn, He showed once again that He could transform Satan's evil schemes into God's glorious triumphs.

The complexity of the characters involved in this intense battle between good and evil only adds to the gripping nature of the story. Satan, the cunning adversary, constantly seeking to deceive and destroy. Jesus, the loving and compassionate Son of God, feeling the weight of the world on His shoulders. Lazarus, the faithful friend, caught in the middle of this spiritual warfare. And John the Baptist, the fearless prophet, martyred for his unwavering faith. Their intertwined stories evoke a range of emotions - from sorrow to anger, from hopelessness to triumph. With a character-rich voice, this tale comes to life, invoking multiple senses and drawing us into the intense drama. We can almost feel the tears streaming down Jesus' face, hear the cries of grief from His followers, and sense the tension between good and evil as it reaches a boiling point. And in the end, we are left in awe of the power and glory of God, who can turn even the darkest of situations into a triumph of His love and grace.

Satan was just getting started, and he planned to use every trick he had up his sleeve to delay and disrupt Jesus' crucifixion. He knew the power of the Jewish laws that governed trials, and he was determined to use them to his advantage. His ultimate goal was to throw a wrench in the fulfillment of Scripture, to spoil the lifelong mission of Jesus. With his cunning ability to confuse and manipulate, Satan was confident he could control the trials and postpone the crucifixion. He relished the thought of Jesus suffering on the cross, but he needed to disrupt the accuracy of Scripture to truly thwart God's plan. And so, he set his devious plan in motion.

But Jesus, knowing the importance of being crucified during this Passover, remained resolute. He was well aware of Satan's tactics and was prepared to face them head on. He was determined to see His mission through to the end, no matter the obstacles that stood in His way. Satan, on the other hand, was counting on the human egos of the corrupt religious leaders to play into his hands. He knew that the more players he could involve, the less likely the crucifixion would take place in the needed time frame. And he had a few tricks up his sleeve to ensure this. He had arranged not one, not two, but six trials in a span of just eight hours. He was determined to drag out the process, to delay and confuse, and ultimately to prevent Jesus from being crucified during the Passover.

As Jesus and His disciples marched through the dusty streets of Jerusalem, a sense of unease hung in the air. The weight of His impending sacrifice weighed heavily on His shoulders, but Jesus pressed on with determination. His piercing eyes scanned the faces of the corrupt religious leaders, their greed and hypocrisy dripping from their every pore. The temple loomed ahead, its grand facade a stark contrast to the darkness within. And as Jesus stepped inside, a wave of righteous fury consumed Him. The sound of jingling coins and haggling voices assaulted His ears as He beheld the chaos before Him. This was meant to be a holy place, a house of prayer, yet it had been transformed into a den of thieves. His voice thundered through the halls as He declared, "My house shall be called a house of prayer, but ye have made it a den of thieves!" With a swift movement, He overturned tables and drove out the money changers. Among them was Annas, the former high priest and father-in-law of Caiaphas, his pockets lined with ill-gotten gains. But Satan chuckled to himself, for he could see his plan unfolding perfectly. Little did he know, Jesus was not one to be swayed by earthly temptations. He was a force to be reckoned with, a being of unwavering strength and conviction. Nothing could deter Him from His ultimate sacrifice. As the dust settled and the chaos subsided, Jesus stood tall and resolute. His eyes blazed with determination and His voice rang out with authority. For He knew that no matter what schemes Satan may devise, His love and sacrifice would always triumph in the end.

Jesus, with His divine knowledge, could see straight into the corrupt hearts of Annas and Caiaphas. He knew they were driven by their own selfish desires, and their thirst for power and control would lead them to do anything to eliminate Him. Jesus also knew that their resentment towards Him would only grow stronger as the week went on. Annas, the conniving and vengeful father-in-law of Caiaphas, would stop at nothing to ensure Jesus' downfall. And Caiaphas, was the high priest and as cunning and calculating as Annas, would blindly follow Annas lead. But Jesus was not intimidated by their schemes, because He had a plan of His own, a trap that would ensure His crucifixion took place as written. Satan, however, was oblivious to the significance of Jesus' outburst in the temple, a calculated move on Jesus' part. He thought he had Jesus right where he wanted Him, rattled and vulnerable. Little did he know, Jesus was always one step ahead. Satan's plan included using some of Jesus' own disciples against Him. He knew that if one of Jesus' followers were involved in His arrest, according to Jewish law, the whole trial would be compromised. Judas, with his strong conviction to make Jesus an earthly leader, fell right into Satan's trap. Little did he know, he was merely a pawn in Satan's game. But Satan's plan didn't end there. He knew the laws and rules of the Jewish court inside and out. According to Jewish law, no arrest could be made for a capital crime at night, and no trial could be held at night. Satan thought he had it all figured out, but he never saw Jesus' trap coming. And, little did Satan know, he was no match for the Son of God. Through it all, Jesus remained steadfast and unwavering. He evoked strong emotions in those around Him, both friend and foe alike. And His voice, filled with authority and compassion, commanded attention and respect. In the end, Satan's schemes were no match for Jesus' divine plan. The crucifixion would take place as it was written, and Jesus would fulfill His purpose on this earth. And even though Satan thought he had the upper hand; he underestimated the power and authority of the Son of God!

CHAPTER 3

WEEK OF THE PASSOVER

Tuesday morning dawned with an air of tension, a heavy weight hanging over the disciples as they gathered around Jesus. Each man could sense the gravity of what was to come, but they were not prepared for what their leader had in store for them. With a commanding presence, Jesus greeted each of the twelve with a personal salutation. His voice, filled with authority and compassion, reached deep into their souls and stirred up a flurry of emotions. To Andrew, He spoke with a sense of urgency, "Be not sorrowed or downcast by the events to come, keep a firm hold on your brothers. For the road ahead will be treacherous, and your strength will be tested." To Peter, He spoke with a tone of warning, "Put not your trust in the force of flesh or weapons of steel. Instead, plant yourself on solid spiritual foundations, and be a rock that you are. For it is not the physical battles that you must prepare for, but the spiritual ones." To James, He spoke with a gentle yet firm voice, "Stay firm in your faith, falter not because of outward appearances, and you shall soon know the reality of that which you believe. For the truth shall always prevail, no matter what trials may come your way." To John, He spoke with a sense of love and tenderness, "Be gentle; love even your enemies; be tolerant, remember that I have trusted you with many things. For your heart is pure, and your love for others shall be your strength." To Nathaniel, He spoke with a sense of wisdom, "Judge not by outward appearances; remain strong in your faith when all appears to leave you; stay committed to your commission as an ambassador of the kingdom. For your faith shall be your shield, and your commitment shall lead you to great things." To Philip, He spoke with a sense of reassurance, "Do not be swayed by the events now impending. Remain firm, even when you cannot see the way; be loyal to your oath of consecration. For your loyalty shall be rewarded, and your faith shall carry you through." To Matthew, He spoke with a sense of gratitude, "Forget not the mercy that granted you passage into the kingdom. Let no man cheat you of your eternal reward. As you have withstood the inclinations of the mortal nature, be willing to be steadfast. For your faithfulness shall be your legacy." To Thomas, He spoke with a sense of encouragement, "No matter how difficult it may be just now, you must walk by faith and not by sight. Doubt not, for I am able to finish the work I have begun, and I shall eventually see all of my faithful ambassadors in the kingdom beyond. For your faith shall be your compass, and your trust in me shall be your strength." To the Alphaeus twins, He spoke with a sense of understanding, "Do not allow the things which you do not understand to crush you; be true to your hearts and put not your trust in either influential men or the changing attitude of the people. Stand by your brothers. For your loyalty to each other shall be your foundation, and your trust in me shall guide you." To Simon Zelotes, He spoke with a sense of hope, "Simon, you may be crushed by disappointment, but your spirit shall rise above all that may come upon you. What you have failed to learn from Me, my spirit will teach you. Seek the true realities of the spirit and cease to be attracted by unreal and material shadows. For your perseverance shall be your strength, and your faith shall guide you." And to Judas Iscariot, He spoke with a sense of love and warning, "Judas, I have loved you and have prayed that you would love your brethren. Be not weary in well-doing, and I would warn you to beware the slippery paths of flattery and the poison darts of ridicule. For your love for your brothers shall be your salvation, and your loyalty to me shall guide you."

Time was now running out before Jesus is betrayed, Jesus departed for Jerusalem with his closest disciples Andrew, Peter, James, and John, while the others set up camp at Gethsemane. This would be their home for the remainder of Jesus' earthly life, a fittingly somber setting for the events that were to unfold. As they made their way down the slope of Olivet, Jesus paused and spent over an hour with the four apostles, his voice rich with emotion as he passionately spoke about the kingdom of God and tried to warn them of the trials and tribulations to come. But their minds were clouded, and they struggled to fully comprehend the gravity of his words.

The night of the Last Supper was fraught with intense tension and turmoil. The air was thick with a sense of impending doom as Satan tempted Judas, his malevolent presence casting a dark cloud over the gathering. He knew that if Jesus was arrested late in the evening, there would be no time for a trial before the Passover, effectively nullifying the Scriptures and all hope for Jesus and his devoted followers.

But Satan was not finished yet, He had a diabolical plan to incite a riot causing chaos during Jesus' arrest. He once again entered Judas, his corrupting influence guiding the Roman soldiers straight to Jesus. But even in the midst of betrayal and chaos, Jesus showed infinite compassion and mercy. When Peter lashed out with his sword, cutting off the high priest's slave's ear, Jesus calmly healed the wound and then turned to Peter, his voice laced with sorrow and determination, "Put your sword back into its sheath. Shall I not drink from the cup of suffering the Father has given me?" And in that moment, it became clear that Jesus was ready to fulfill his destiny as foretold in the Scriptures.

But for his disciples, He was still a complex and intriguing character, their minds struggling to reconcile the powerful and miraculous leader they knew with the humble and submissive man before them. But as the night wore on, emotions ran high. Fear, confusion, and anger filled the hearts of Jesus' followers as they tried to make sense of the events unfolding before them. And in the midst of it all, Jesus remained steadfast and resolute, His voice rich with emotion as He spoke of His imminent sacrifice and the ultimate plan of salvation for all. In this complex and intriguing tale, the characters were all embroiled in their own struggles and motivations.

But it was Satan, the ultimate antagonist, who constantly tried to disrupt God's plan and lead Jesus astray. And as the night wore on, the characters were consumed by strong emotions, their senses heightened by the intensity of the moment. Indeed, this was a night that evoked multiple senses, the smell of fear and sweat, the taste of betrayal and bitterness, the sound of voices raised in confusion and desperation, and the touch of a hand healing a wound. But above all, it was the rich and emotional voice of Jesus that rang out, a beacon of hope in the darkness, a reminder that even in the face of betrayal and suffering, salvation was at hand.

CHAPTER 4

THE HIGH PRIEST DEMANDS DEATH

As the early morning hours crept in, the atmosphere in the chamber grew tense. The first of six trials was about to begin, and all eyes were on Jesus as he was brought before Annas, the former chief priest. He was humble and still as he stood before the man he had embarrassed in front of his esteemed religious peers. Annas, with a wicked glint in his eye, relished the power he now held over Jesus. He had been waiting for this moment, to exact revenge on the man who had humiliated him and challenged his authority.

The sound of hushed whispers filled the room, as the onlookers eagerly awaited the unfolding of the trial. The flickering torches cast eerie shadows on the walls, adding to the ominous atmosphere. Annas, feeling exceedingly important, sat on his throne, a cruel smile playing on his lips. He was determined to make Jesus pay for his insolence, and he relished the thought of finally having him at his mercy. His once gentle features were now twisted with anger and malice, making him appear more like a demon than a religious leader. As Jesus stood before him, his eyes were filled with sorrow and pain. He knew what fate awaited him, but he also knew that he must endure it for the sake of humanity.

Despite the physical and emotional turmoil he was facing, his spirit remained unbroken, and his resolve only grew stronger. The tension in the room was palpable, as the two men faced each other, one driven by revenge and the other by love and sacrifice. The clash of their opposing motivations created a powerful and complex dynamic, making the scene all the more intriguing.

As the trial began, the emotions in the room reached a fever pitch. The voices rose, the accusations flew, and the tension reached its breaking point. It was a battle of wills, a battle of good versus evil. And in that moment, all eyes were on Jesus, the man who would soon be crucified for the sins of humanity. In this moment, the characters were more than just ordinary men, they were forces to be reckoned with. Their actions and emotions evoked strong feelings in those around them, making the scene all the more intense. As the trial continued, the character rich voices of both Annas and Jesus echoed through the chamber, each one vying for dominance.

It was a battle of wits, a battle for power, and a battle for the fate of one man. In this one moment, multiple senses were invoked, as the sights, sounds, and smells of the scene came alive. And in the end, it was a battle that would shape the course of history, leaving an indelible mark on the hearts and minds of all who witnessed it.

He started the grilling by bombarding Jesus with questions about His loyal band of followers, but Jesus refused to engage in discussing such trivial matters with Annas. Instead, he calmly turned the tables and probed Annas about His teachings, subtly pointing out that as the esteemed high priest and revered religious leader of the Jews, he should already be well versed in what Jesus preached. With a composed demeanor, Jesus reminded Annas, "I have spoken openly and fearlessly to the world; I have always taught in the synagogue and in the temple, where all the Jews gather. I have said nothing in secret. Why question me? Ask those who heard me. Surely, they know what I said." As the tension in the room thickened, the air was filled with the smell of fear and apprehension.

Annas, the sly and cunning religious authority, now stood face to face with Jesus, the enigmatic and controversial figure. The clash of wills and ideologies between these two powerful men was palpable, sending chills down the spine of anyone who bore witness to the scene. With every word that Jesus spoke, a sense of awe and reverence filled the room. His voice, rich with authority and wisdom, commanded the attention of all in the room. As the interrogation continued, it became clear that this was no ordinary man, but someone who possessed a power and presence beyond human understanding. The intensity of the moment was overwhelming, as the fate of Jesus hung in the balance. Jesus' hands were bound tightly behind His back, the ropes digging deep into His flesh, as He stood in front of Annas. The room was filled with the stench of fear and anger, the tension so thick you could cut it with a knife.

Annas, a powerful and corrupt leader, was seething with rage as he glared at Jesus, his eyes filled with malicious intent. This whole situation was a mockery of justice, a blatant violation of the law. Annas had no right to put Jesus on trial, let alone in front of only one Judge, himself. There were no witnesses, no proper procedure, and yet Annas acted as if he held the power of life and death over Jesus. But Jesus stood tall, His gaze steady and unwavering. He knew the truth, and He refused to be intimidated by Annas' false authority. In fact, He seemed to be the one judging Annas with His piercing stare, making the corrupt leader squirm under His scrutiny. Annas was beside himself with fury. He had never encountered someone like Jesus before. He was used to dealing with cowards and liars, but this man stood before him with a quiet confidence that unsettled him. In a fit of rage, Annas ordered his men to whip Jesus, as Annas smirked, "Now, who is in control?" But even as the lashes tore through Jesus' flesh, He didn't cry out or beg for mercy. Instead, He looked at Annas with pity, as if Annas was the one being judged by a higher power. The whole scene was chaotic, Jesus remained a mysterious and enigmatic figure, shrouded in strength and resilience.

Emotions ran high, with fear, anger, and confusion swirling in the minds of those present. And yet, amidst it all, Jesus remained calm and composed, his character unshaken by the relentless questioning. As the interrogation came to a close, one thing was certain: this encounter would be remembered for years to come. The clash of these two complex and intriguing characters had left an indelible mark on all who bore witness, and the echoes of their words and actions would continue to resonate long after they parted ways.

As the night dragged on, the darkness seemed to suffocate the streets of Jerusalem. The moon hid behind a thick blanket of clouds, casting a dark and troubling shadow over the city. It was the perfect cover for the sinister plan that was about to unfold. Caiaphas, the high priest, sat in his opulent house, surrounded by a group of men. They were plotting in the dead of night, breaking every law and tradition. The air was thick with tension and malice, as they eagerly awaited the arrival of their victim. At 3:30 a.m., Jesus was brought before them, a mere pawn in their twisted game. The sight of his beaten and weary form only fueled their cruel intentions. They knew it was illegal, but they didn't care. This was a kangaroo court, a sham of a trial, orchestrated by a clash of good and evil, light and darkness. And in that moment, Satan seemed to have the upper hand. But little did he know that this was just the beginning of a much bigger plan. A plan that would ultimately lead to his defeat and the redemption of mankind.

The witnesses on hand were vehemently contradicting each other, their voices rising in a cacophony of chaos. Caiaphas, the high priest, felt his patience wearing thin as he desperately tried to make sense of the conflicting testimonies. He needed to get this case down to Pilate, to wash his hands of this troublesome affair. But his father-in-law, Annas, had other plans. He wanted this man, Jesus, dead. And Caiaphas knew that he had no legitimate witnesses to support his case. Frustrated and desperate, Caiaphas resorted to illegal means. He approached the accused himself, trying to extract a confession from this man who had caused so much commotion in Jerusalem. But to his surprise, Jesus remained silent, a calm and unwavering presence amidst the chaos. Finally, Caiaphas asked the question that would seal Jesus' fate: "Are you the Christ, the Son of the Blessed?" The answer that came was like a thunderbolt, shaking Caiaphas to his core. "I am," Jesus declared, his voice ringing with authority. "And you will see the Son of man sitting on the right hand of power and coming in the clouds of Heaven."

Caiaphas was taken aback. This man was claiming to be God? But what he didn't realize was that Jesus was offering a prophecy, one that he couldn't possibly understand in his limited human capacity. As the first two trials came to a close, Jesus stood before the Sanhedrin, the highest court of the Jews. But in the darkness of night, their verdict held no weight in the eyes of the Romans. It wasn't until Jesus stood before Pilate, the ruler of Judea, that a final judgment could be made. In the eyes of the Sanhedrin, Jesus was guilty of treason, of attempting to overthrow the government. And in their minds, there was no doubt. With Nicodemus the only one to remain silent, they voted unanimously to take Jesus to Pilate, their minds made up. But little did they know that Jesus had already sealed his fate, willingly surrendering himself to the ultimate sacrifice for the sake of all mankind. And as the law of the Medes and Persians, unchangeable and irrevocable, declared him guilty, Jesus prepared to carry his cross to Calvary, his love for humanity shining brighter than the sun.

The night was long and torturous, with Christ on full display while Satan reveled in his apparent control. Time was on his side, with the hours ticking by and no one willing to make a decision. Even Nicodemus and Joseph, who had argued for Jesus' innocence, seemed to be under Satan's sway. As the sun threatened to rise, Pilate's permission was still needed to proceed with the crucifixion, but he remained blind to Christ's guilt. It appeared that Satan's plan to stall the crucifixion at the last moment was succeeding. By daybreak, Christ was still being dragged from one judge to another, a mere shell of his former self. His body was weak from the brutal beatings, his blood staining the ground, and his mind exhausted from sleep deprivation and dehydration. And yet, the worst was yet to come.

It was 6:30 a.m. and Pilate, weary of the case, sent Jesus to be tried by Herod Antipas across town. Herod, known for his cruelty and beheading of John the Baptist, was sure to deal with this problem swiftly. But Herod saw Jesus as nothing more than a magician, a sideshow act to be mocked and ridiculed. He wanted to be entertained, to see Jesus perform a miracle. When Jesus refused, Herod and his court treated him as a mere jester, a clown to be dressed up and paraded around. And then, just as quickly as he had arrived, Jesus was sent back to Pilate, a mockery of a king.

As the morning light shone upon the tortured and humiliated Christ, it was clear that the forces of evil were at work. The characters in this twisted tale were complex and intriguing, each with their own motivations and agendas. And as the events unfolded, a tumult of emotions rose within those who witnessed it all. It was a scene that would forever be etched in their minds, a testament to the power of good versus evil, and the ultimate sacrifice that Christ would make.

"Now back at the palace, Pilate could finally relax and enjoy his breakfast. He had just made a difficult decision, but it was over now. Or so he thought. As he gazed out of his window, he saw the commotion in the square below. His heart skipped a beat when he saw Jesus, the man he had just sent across town, being dragged back, bound and dressed in a mocking robe. Pilate's mind raced, trying to understand what was happening. But it was clear that Herod, the man he had hoped would take this situation off his hands, was in no mood to cooperate. With Satan's influence tainting his thoughts, Pilate desperately tried to find a way out of this verdict. His first attempt was to offer a compromise to the chief priests. He would have Jesus chastised and beaten and then release him. But the priests, consumed by their hatred for Jesus, refused.

His next idea was to use a custom of releasing a prisoner on the Passover. And who better to put next to Jesus than Barabbas, a notorious criminal? Barabbas, who was guilty of treason, had committed a capital crime and was awaiting crucifixion. Surely the crowd would choose Jesus over him. But to Pilate's surprise, the plan backfired. The high priests, scribes, and Sanhedrin all demanded that Jesus be crucified, their voices echoing through the streets. Satan's victory was snatched from his grasp, and yet he still couldn't comprehend the significance of Jesus' outburst in the temple earlier that week.

Left with only one option, Satan's rage and desperation grew. He wanted to beat Jesus to death before the cross. And so, he gathered a whole band of soldiers and began to strip Jesus of his clothes. They placed a scarlet robe on his bruised and battered body, mocking him as a king. A crown of thorns was pressed onto his head, and a reed was placed in his hand. As they bowed down and spat at him, they sneered, "Hail, King of the Jews!" And with each blow to his head, each spit on his face, they led him away to be crucified. The scene was chaotic and vile, but there was something else in the air. A tangible sense of evil and darkness that seemed to seep into the very souls of those present.

As Satan's plan unfolded, the emotions of the crowd were a mixture of fear, hatred, and confusion. And yet, amidst the chaos, Jesus remained calm and resolute. His character, complex and mysterious, shone through even in his darkest hour. And as he walked towards his fate, his voice rang out with a strength and grace that left the soldiers and the crowd in awe. This was not just a man being led to his death, this was the Son of God, willingly sacrificing himself for the sins of the world. And as the soldiers led him away, the weight of their actions began to sink in. But it was too late for them to turn back now. The wheels had been set in motion, and there was no stopping the events that would lead to Jesus' crucifixion. The darkness had taken hold, and Satan's influence was stronger than ever. But little did he know, his defeat was already in motion. The cross, the very instrument of Jesus' death, would soon become the symbol of his ultimate victory."

As the throngs of people swarmed towards the gruesome spectacle of the crucifixion, the air was thick with a tangible sense of foreboding. The sound of pounding footsteps and frenzied whispers filled the streets, as the crowd pushed and shoved in their desperation to catch a glimpse of the condemned man. Jesus, his body battered and bruised beyond recognition, trudged wearily through the sea of humanity. His face, once radiant and full of love, now bore the marks of unspeakable torture. Yet, in the midst of his suffering, there was a fierce determination in his eyes, a resilience that refused to be broken. The weight of the cross bore down on Jesus with a crushing force, threatening to crush his spirit as well. But with every step, he summoned all of his willpower to keep moving forward, to fulfill his destiny. Every labored breath, every drop of blood, was a testament to his unyielding strength and unwavering love.

And as the onlookers watched in awe and horror, they could not help but be drawn to this enigmatic figure, this man who radiated both agony and grace. For in his suffering, Jesus had become something more, something beyond human comprehension. And though they may not have understood it at the time, the people were witnessing a divine sacrifice, a love that transcended all pain and suffering. As he stumbled and faltered, his inner strength and determination were the only things driving him on. The onlookers could sense his sheer exhaustion radiating from him, a tangible wave of weariness and pain. They watched as he stumbled, his clothes torn and tattered, his feet bloody and blistered. And in that moment, they couldn't help but feel a deep sense of sympathy for this man who had endured so much.

But as the procession continued towards the place of execution, the atmosphere changed. The once somber mood shifted to one of frenzied excitement, the crowds growing more restless and boisterous. From the rooftops and the streets, they watched with morbid fascination as Jesus was led to his fate. They couldn't tear their eyes away, caught up in the fervor of the moment. But amidst the chaos and the noise, there were those who couldn't help but feel a twinge of guilt and remorse. They realized too late the gravity of what they had been a part of. The weight of their actions now bearing down on them with unbearable intensity. Tears streamed down their faces as they watched Jesus suffer, his body broken and beaten. And in that moment, they couldn't help but feel a deep sense of regret and remorse for what they had done. The man they had once mocked and ridiculed now lay before them, a symbol of love and sacrifice.

They had been swept up in the frenzy, but now, as they looked upon the man who had done nothing but spread love and compassion, they couldn't help but question their actions. Had they been too quick to judge? Too eager to join in the crowd? As Jesus finally reached the hill where he would be crucified, the once lively crowd fell silent. The only sound that could be heard was the hammering of nails as they were driven into his hands and feet. And in that moment, a sense of overwhelming sorrow and grief washed over the onlookers. The air was heavy with emotion as the crowd dispersed, each person left to grapple with their own inner turmoil. And though the deed was done, the memory of that fateful day would forever haunt them, a constant reminder of the power of one man's unwavering love and the overwhelming weight of their own actions.

Amidst the chaos and turmoil, one voice rose above the rest. It was a voice of pure love and forgiveness, cutting through the darkness with a fierce intensity. It was the voice of Jesus, in the midst of his suffering, speaking words that shook the very foundations of those who heard them. As he stumbled and fell under the weight of his cross, Jesus looked into the eyes of his tormentors and spoke with a calm and unwavering strength. His words were like a balm to their troubled souls, and they couldn't help but be moved by his unwavering love and compassion. But not everyone was touched by Jesus' words. Some of the people jeered and mocked him, their hearts hardened by hatred and fear. Others were silent, their minds racing with conflicting emotions. And there were those who turned their heads and dabbed their eyes, unable to bear witness to such a pure and selfless act of sacrifice. As Jesus continued to carry his cross, his body bruised and broken from the relentless beatings, the true power and strength of this humble man was revealed. He was not just a mere mortal, but a divine being, willing to endure unimaginable pain and suffering for the sake of others. And in that moment, as he hung upon the cross, the hearts and minds of those who bore witness to his crucifixion were forever changed. For they had seen the face of true love and sacrifice, and it would stay with them for the rest of their lives.

But the battle was not yet over. As Jesus hung upon the cross, he was now unprotected and at the mercy of Satan's brutality. And yet, even in the face of such unimaginable evil, he remained steadfast in his commitment to the mission. With every step he took, with every breath he struggled to take, Jesus showed the world His love and commitment. He was their Savior who was not defined by strength or power, but by love and sacrifice. And in the end, it was this love that conquered all, forever changing the hearts and minds of those who witnessed it.

Satan, the master manipulator, reveled in every blow and lash that struck Jesus' flesh. His cruel laughter echoed through the air as he relished in the sight of Jesus' body writhing in agony. With every strike, Satan's grip on victory tightened, for if Jesus died before the cross, all would be lost. But Satan was not satisfied with just physical torment. No, he aimed to break Jesus in every possible way. He orchestrated each beating and flogging with a devastating force, intent on causing death. And as the blows rained down, Jesus' body was ravaged beyond recognition. His lungs filled with blood, his spleen ruptured, and his kidneys battered, all from the brutal force of the blows. But it wasn't just physical pain that Jesus endured. His spirit was drained, his energy depleted. He suffered from dehydration and blood loss, his body weakened and on the brink of collapse. The abuse inflicted by Satan and his minions had taken its toll, and Jesus was desperately close to death.

And then, in a final act of cruelty, Satan caused Jesus to stumble and fall. The carpenter of Nazareth, who had carried many beams on his shoulders before, was now unable to lift himself from the ground. Someone kicked him while he was down, but Jesus could not move. He lay there, broken and battered, a symbol of the ultimate sacrifice he was about to make. As the scene unfolded, onlookers could feel the weight of the moment, the intensity of the suffering, the sound of agonized cries filled their ears. But amidst all the chaos and pain, one thing was clear: Satan's grip on victory was slipping, for even in his weakest moment, Jesus remained steadfast in his mission to his Love toward mankind.. His humanity was utterly drained, leaving him weak and vulnerable. The centurion, a strong and stoic man, found himself at a loss. He couldn't burden his soldiers with the task of carrying the cross, nor could he ask a Jew to do it, for fear of defiling them and preventing them from partaking in their holy Passover. As the column marched towards Calvary, a man named Simon of Cyrene appeared. Fresh from the country, he was simply going about his day when he stumbled upon the procession. He stopped to see what was happening, his curiosity piqued. The centurion's sharp eyes immediately fell upon him. This man, Simon, was the perfect candidate. With a sharp command, the legionnaires seized Simon and forced him to bear the weight of Jesus' cross. In that fleeting moment, time seemed to stand still as Simon stepped onto the pages of history. As he helped Jesus to his feet, he felt the weight of the cross upon his own shoulders. He couldn't comprehend the magnitude of what was transpiring, but he could see the determination etched on Jesus' face. It was a look that spoke volumes, conveying the urgency of reaching the cross before it was too late. The fate of all humanity rested on this moment. As their eyes met, Simon could sense the depth of suffering and sorrow within Jesus. Yet, he also saw a glimmer of hope and unwavering strength. In that moment, Simon knew he had to help Jesus reach his destination. With every step, he could feel the weight of the cross and the weight of the world upon his shoulders. And as they finally reached Calvary, Simon realized the true purpose of this journey. By helping Jesus, he had become a part of the greatest story ever told. Jesus lay on the cross, His body wracked with pain and His heart heavy with sorrow. The weight of the world's sins bore down on Him, and yet He remained steadfast in His purpose. Every breath was a struggle, every movement a torment. Yet, through it all, Jesus wore a serene smile on His lips, a quiet confidence in His eyes. The sound of jeering and mocking filled the air, as Satan and his followers reveled in their perceived victory. But as Jesus hung there, close to death, He shouted the words that would change everything: Tetelestai "It is finished." In that moment, Satan knew he had been defeated. The weight of his schemes and temptations, the darkness that had threatened to consume the world, all came crashing down around him. And in the face of it all, Jesus simply smiled. But it was not a smile of gloating or triumph. It was a smile of love and sacrifice, a smile that spoke of a greater purpose fulfilled. And as

Satan slunk away, defeated and broken, the heavens rejoiced at the ultimate victory of good over evil. Yes, Jesus may have been near death and under immense suffering, but He never wavered. His strength and resilience in the face of such darkness and pain only served to make His sacrifice all the more powerful. The soldiers marched Him up the hill of Calvary, where He was to be crucified like a lamb led to slaughter. But Satan, ever persistent, was not ready to give up yet. He goaded the soldiers to mock Jesus, taunting Him with the words, "If you are the King of the Jews, save yourself!" Satan knew that Jesus had the power to save Himself, and he wanted to see if He would use it. But Satan's temptations did not end there. As Jesus hung on the cross, Satan entered the body of a Roman soldier and used him to mock and tempt Jesus one last time. "If you are the Son of God, save yourself and come down from there," the soldier jeered. These were the same words Satan had used to tempt Jesus throughout His life - "Prove to the world who you are." But Jesus, in His infinite love and mercy, did not give in to Satan's temptations. He remained on the cross, enduring the pain and humiliation, so that all of humanity could be saved. And as He hung there, weeping and bleeding, He showed us the true meaning of sacrifice and Love… and in that moment, as He breathed His last breath, the world was forever changed.

CHAPTER 5

JESUS' BODY

After Christ took his last breath, the atmosphere was thick with sorrow and defeat. The weight of his death hung heavily in the air, as if the world itself was mourning. But amidst the grief, two men emerged from the shadows, their faces hidden behind the veils of wealth and power. Joseph of Arimathea and Nicodemus, members of the prestigious Sanhedrin party, stepped forward and made a request that would change the course of history. It was a noble gesture, to ask for the body of Christ, but it raises a question. Why did these two men, feel compelled to claim his body when his own family did not? It seems almost too convenient. And as the two men carefully prepared the body for burial, Satan was watching and waiting, circling the earth like a hungry predator. For the first time, the body of Christ was in the hands of the very people who had condemned him to death, the Sanhedrin. These were the same men who had voted for his crucifixion, the men who were supposed to be the religious leaders of Israel. And Satan saw an opportunity, a chance to strike at the heart of God's plan. He entered both men, tempting them with every sin imaginable. Greed, lust, wisdom, power. He played on their vanity, whispering in their ears that they deserved some reward for their role in the Burial of this revered prophet. He planted the seed of doubt, suggesting that they could somehow gain the powers of Christ by keeping something from his body, a lock of hair or a nail clipping. Satan knew the Scriptures well, and he knew that Christ was meant to rise from the dead in three days. His future plans depended on convincing the world that this was a lie, that Christ had not risen at all, but rather, that his body had been stolen by his followers. And so, he orchestrated the placement of Jesus' body into Joseph's private tomb, with the help of two Jewish religious leaders who could later confirm that the body was indeed dead and missing or had been stolen by the eleven. But let's not forget the eleven disciples, who Satan was counting on for this lie. These were the same men who had fled in fear when Jesus was arrested, leaving their faith in question. And yet, we are expected to believe that they were brave and capable enough to overpower the Roman guards and take Jesus' body from the tomb? It's a ludicrous notion, and yet, somehow, Satan has managed to deceive the world with this lie. He counts on our doubts and our fears, on our willingness to believe the worst in others. And so, the truth of Christ's resurrection becomes obscured, buried under a mountain of deception. But let us not be fooled. Let us remember the eleven disciples who deserted Christ and yet were transformed into fearless leaders after his resurrection. Let us remember the power of God, who conquered death and defeated Satan once and for all. And let us never forget the truth, that Christ rose from the dead, and nothing can ever change that.

CHAPTER 6

SIMON OF CYRENE WEEKS PRIOR TO THE CRUCIFIXION

As the early morning sun rose, Simon of Cyrene was filled with excitement for the journey ahead to Jerusalem. The Passover festivities were always a sight to behold and this year, he was accompanied by his eldest son, Alexander. The long trip from Cyrene to Jerusalem awaited them, so they needed to embark on their journey. Simon was eager to share the Passover traditions with his son, hoping to deepen his understanding of the Scriptures. Unfortunately, his younger son Rufus had to stay behind with their mother. Simon could sense Alexander's desire for Rufus to join them, but he was impressed by his son's maturity in not causing a fuss about it. This trip would provide the perfect opportunity for them to bond and discuss the significance of Passover week, the miraculous exodus from Egypt, and the protection of the Jews by the blood-stained doors. Simon was always seeking to gain a deeper understanding of the Scriptures and the promised Savior, so he could effectively pass it on to his sons. He was afraid of not being a good role model for Alexander and Rufus. Having made this journey before, Simon knew of an inn just outside of Jerusalem where they could rest. He was determined to reach there in time for the Passover feast, but with an extra traveler this time, anything could happen on the long journey. Alexander, who had turned twelve a few months ago, was a remarkable young man. He was tall for his age and possessed great wisdom. He always strived to bring joy to his parents. Alexander was excited to witness the Passover celebrations and was eager to see Jesus, who was rumored to be in the area. Both Simon and Alexander had heard of the powerful miracles performed by Jesus, and they couldn't wait to experience it for themselves. They traveled light, their footsteps quick and urgent as they made their way through the dusty roads. The sun beat down on them, a constant reminder of the danger that lurked in the shadows. They had left their donkey behind, not wanting to attract any unwanted attention. It was just the two of them, Simon and Alexander, carrying only the bare necessities - food, water, and the weight of their shared excitement. For Simon, this was a familiar journey, one he had made countless times before. But for Alexander, every step was filled with a sense of wonder and adventure. He had never been outside of his small village, never experienced the thrill of exploration. And on this trip, he would finally see the grand city of Jerusalem. As they walked, Simon's voice was alive with tales of their destination. Simon spoke of the bustling streets, the vibrant markets, and the magnificent temples. He painted a picture so vivid that Alexander could almost feel the scorching sun on his skin and smell the exotic spices in the air. But there was also a hint of caution in Simon's voice, a reminder that danger lurked at every corner. They had to be careful, watchful, and always on guard. For Alexander, this only added to the excitement, the thrill of the unknown. As they reached the outskirts of Jerusalem, Simon's pace quickened, his excitement growing with every step. And then, they were there, standing at the gates of the grandest city Alexander had ever seen. But as they entered the crowded streets, Alexander could feel a sense of unease creeping up on him. The crowds were overwhelming, the noise and chaos almost suffocating. Yet, he couldn't help but be drawn in by the energy and excitement of the people around him. Simon urged him to stay close, to not get lost in the sea of bodies. And as they made their way through the streets, Alexander couldn't help but marvel at the sights and sounds around him. This was a city like no other, filled with life, color, and a sense of wonder that he had never experienced before. Little did he know, this would be the last day he would spend with Simon. The last day before his life would be forever changed. But for now, he was caught up in the moment, swept away by the magic of Jerusalem. And as the day turned into night, they settled down under the stars, warmed by the crackling campfire, their hearts full of anticipation for the adventures that awaited them tomorrow.

The air was thick with tension, a palpable buzz that seemed to vibrate through the crowd. People were pushing and shoving, their voices rising in panic and confusion. Something was definitely wrong. And then, the news spread like wildfire: Jesus had been arrested. Simon felt a surge of fear and urgency, and he grabbed Alexander's hand, pulling him through the throngs of people. As they drew closer, they saw that the crowd had come to a standstill. A group of soldiers surrounded a figure on the ground, their weapons drawn and their voices barking out orders. Simon's heart raced as he pushed through the crowd, desperate to get a closer look. But then, the centurion's eyes meet his, and time seemed to slow down. The soldier's voice was sharp and commanding, but Simon couldn't make out the words. He clutched onto Alexander, trying to hold him back, but the guards were pulling him towards the man on the ground. And then, the unthinkable happened. The centurion ordered Simon to pick up the cross and carry it. Simon's mind raced, his eyes darting between his son and the cross. "No," he cried out, "I can't leave my son." But the guards were relentless, pushing him down with Jesus on the ground. The crowd surged around them, their cries and screams echoing in Simon's ears. He couldn't tear his eyes away from the man on the ground, his features contorted in pain. In that moment, everything changed.

Alexander stood there, frozen in shock and horror, as he watched his father Simon being forced to carry the cross for Jesus. At first, Simon had been hesitant, worried about leaving his son behind. But as he looked into Jesus' eyes, something changed. Suddenly, Simon was filled with compassion and concern for the man before him. He called out to Alexander, "Follow us, son. Stay close." But Jesus remained silent, and Simon continued to answer Him, determined to get Him to the cross before He died. Alexander followed along, his heart racing as he watched the blood flowing from Jesus' open wounds. With each step Jesus took, the weight of the cross seemed to grow heavier, and he stumbled and fell multiple times. But Simon was always there to help him up, never once faltering in his determination to see Jesus to the end. As they reached the top of the hill, the Roman soldiers ordered Simon to drop the cross and leave. Alexander watched in terror as Jesus looked into his father's eyes once more, and without saying a word, warned him of the evil that awaited him. Simon asked why he was being targeted, why he was in danger. And in that moment, he made a plea to protect his sons and his wife. Tears streamed down Alexander's face as he watched his father being pushed away from Jesus, the man he was willing to give his life for. But Alexander didn't understand why. Jesus never complained, never fought back, but instead prayed for forgiveness for those who had put Him on the cross. And then, one of the

Roman soldiers taunted Him, challenging Him to save Himself if He truly was the Son of God. The day had started off so beautifully, but now everything had gone terribly wrong. Alexander was grateful that his brother Rufus had stayed behind, even though he had been disappointed at the time. He now realized that it was for the best. This was the last day he would ever spend with his father. And what he would witness, he could never bring himself to tell Rufus or his mother. It was a burden he would carry with him to the grave.

Simon dragged Alexander away from the chaos, his heart pounding with fear and determination. The crowds jostled and pressed, their deafening clamor drowning out all attempts at conversation. But Simon refused to give up. He had to make Alexander understand. "Listen to me, son!" he cried, his voice strained and urgent. "This man Jesus is no ordinary man.

He is the Savior, the Son of the living God, the one spoken about in the Scriptures. I saw His glory, felt His power, the moment I looked into His eyes. He promised me that you and Rufus will be protected, that you will become fishers of men. But you must follow the Scriptures, for they have been fulfilled today by Jesus. And this blood on me," he gestured to his stained clothes, "it is shed for you, for your brother, your mother, me, and the entire world. Remember this day, Alexander. Remember the sacrifice Jesus made for you." Tears streamed down Alexander's face, his entire body trembling with fear and confusion. "But Father, I don't want you to go!" he cried out, clinging to Simon's hand. "I have to, my son," Simon replied, his voice heavy with sorrow. "The Evil One seeks me, and I must lead him away from you and our family. You must go home and take care of them, reminding them constantly of Jesus and His love." As Simon spoke, a shiver ran down his spine. He knew the danger that awaited him in the coming hours. Jesus had warned him, but He also knew that in just a few short hours, He would be dead. And for the next three days, Simon's life would be in grave danger. With a heavy heart, Simon made the difficult decision to leave his family and seek refuge in the countryside. But before he left, he pleaded one last time with Alexander. "Please, my son, go home and take care of our family. Tell Rufus about this day, about Jesus and His love. I will join you soon." And with a heavy heart and a sense of gloom, Simon of Cyrene left town, his destiny forever changed by his encounter with the Son of God. But little did he know that this was just the beginning of his journey, for Satan had taken notice of Simon and vowed revenge for his role in helping Jesus make it to the cross. And for the next three days, Simon would have to endure unimaginable trials and danger as he waited for Jesus to rise from the dead. But his mission was not over yet. He was now a part of the greatest story ever told, a story of sacrifice, redemption, and love. And his voice would forever echo through the ages, a testament to the power of faith and the enduring legacy of Jesus Christ.

CHAPTER 7

SATAN TEMPTS JOSEPH AND NICODEMUS

It was high noon in Jerusalem, the blistering sun beating down on the bustling city. But suddenly, a darkness descended upon the land, as if the very heavens were mourning. The ground began to shake violently, sending people running for cover as the earth split open and graves were torn asunder. But amidst the chaos, something even more shocking occurred. The curtain in the temple, the holiest of places, was torn in two from top to bottom. It was as if God Himself had reached down and ripped it apart, a powerful display of divine wrath. As the people stood in awe, trying to make sense of the inexplicable events, the soldiers watching Jesus couldn't help but make crude jokes. They mocked about His robe, saying it must hold some mystical powers, they say He has healed the sick, commanded demons to come out of the people, and even brought the dead back to life. But as they continued to jest, a sinister presence crept into their minds. It was Satan himself, filling them with a feverish obsession for Jesus' clothing. Rumors began to spread like wildfire, whispered furtively among the soldiers. Some claimed that Jesus possessed a magic medallion sewn into the lining of His garment, a gift from the prophet Elijah. The soldiers, now consumed with greed and curiosity, coveted Jesus' clothes, desperate to discover the source of His power. But little did they know, it was not some trinket or talisman that granted Jesus His abilities, but the strength of God His Father. In this moment of darkness and turmoil, the true power of Jesus was revealed, and the soldiers could not help but be drawn in by its all-consuming force. With all the frenzied commotion over the garments, it became necessary to draw lots for them. The victorious soldier, known as Marcus the Blood Drinker for his insatiable thirst for animal sacrifice, now stood before Jesus on the cross. With a sardonic grin, he taunted, "If you truly are the Son of God, come down from there and save yourself. That would prove to the world who you truly are, and maybe I'll even return your robe to you." He chuckled, relishing the thought of his own cunning. But deep within, Marcus couldn't help but yearn for the possibility of an even greater reward - the robe could make him a wealthy man. As he watched Jesus dying, he couldn't help but think, I didn't think you could come down, but it was worth a try. Marcus had no inkling of the truth - that the robe he now possessed was coveted by none other than Satan himself. And his brief ownership of it would soon come to a violent and abrupt end. Meanwhile, Jesus, with mere moments left to live, spent them in prayer for the world. As he felt his last bit of strength slipping away, he uttered, (tetelestai) or "It is finished." And with his final breath, he surrendered himself, whispering, "Into thy hands I commit my spirit." But this story is not just about Marcus and his schemes, or even Jesus's selfless sacrifice alone but it is a tale of darkness and light, of good and evil, of hope and despair. As the blood dripped from Jesus' wounds and his body grew cold, the world stood still in awe and fear. And in that moment, a new chapter began - one that would change the course of history and ignite a flame of faith that would never be extinguished.

As the earth began to tremble and quake, the people scattered across the peak of Skull Mountain, desperately seeking safety. Little did they know, there was nowhere to hide from God.

The commanding soldier ordered the legs of the criminals to be broken, hastening their deaths. While the two on either side of Jesus had their legs shattered, the soldiers were surprised to find that Jesus was already dead. In order to confirm this, they were instructed to pierce His side. Thus, Jesus was declared deceased. With the Jews eagerly preparing for their grand religious festival, they were meticulous in preparations and could not allow dead bodies to remain hanging on the cross during their sacred Passover ceremony, which was ironic but meant to honor God.

Now that Jesus was dead and Satan's attempts to stop the crucifixion had failed, he set his sights on gaining access to the body of Christ. Satan had been keeping a close eye on Joseph and Nicodemus, two influential members of the Sanhedrin, who had shown sympathy towards Jesus. As Joseph of Arimathea and Nicodemus watched from the outskirts of the crowd, their hearts sank at the sight of Jesus being brutally crucified. They were both respected members of the Jewish community, well-versed in the laws and customs of their people, and they knew that this was a grave injustice. They tried to intervene, to use their knowledge and influence to stop the crucifixion, but their attempts were met with failure. Satan, ever the cunning adversary, used this moment to tempt both men to do something that would have been unthinkable just a short time earlier, to stooped to the level of taking something from Jesus' body, like his hair that Satan could use later. He knew that these two men, driven by compassion for Jesus, could be his pawns in a greater scheme. And so, as the nails were being driven into Jesus' hands and feet, Satan whispered in Joseph's ear. He knew that Joseph, a wealthy and prominent council member, could approach Pilate and convene a meeting on short notice. And so, while Jesus was still suffering on the cross, Joseph of Arimathea boldly stepped forward and requested his body.

Nicodemus, a Pharisee and member of the Sanhedrin, offered his assistance as well, despite the risk to his high status and reputation in the Jewish community. As they stood before Pilate, Joseph and Nicodemus could feel the weight of their actions. They knew that this could jeopardize everything they had worked for, but they also knew that it was the right thing to do. Joseph, in particular, showed great courage in going before Pilate and requesting Jesus' body. Little did he know that his actions fulfilled a prophecy written hundreds of years before, *"And they made His grave with the wicked, but with the rich at His death, because He had done no violence, nor was any deceit in His mouth" (Isaiah 53:8)*. Joseph was a wealthy and successful man, accustomed to living a life of luxury and comfort. He had been a secret supporter of Jesus, but he feared the backlash of openly standing with him. He could hardly be called a true follower of Christ at this point, but his respect for Jesus was enough for Satan to exploit. And so, in this moment, Joseph of Arimathea became a key player in the ultimate sacrifice of Jesus. As the two men laid Jesus' body in the tomb, they were filled with a mixture of sorrow and confusion. They couldn't fully comprehend the events that had just taken place, but they knew that something significant had happened. And little did they know their small acts of compassion would be remembered as a crucial role in the greatest story ever told. Joseph stood before Pilate; his mind consumed with conflicting thoughts. He had spent his entire life devoted to his religious beliefs, but now he found himself tempted by the promises of power and wealth. The weight of his decision hung heavily upon him as he argued for the body of Jesus to be placed in his tomb. He had heard of the miracles that Jesus had performed and had been drawn to the clarity of His teachings. But as a respected leader in the community, Joseph knew the consequences of publicly declaring himself as a disciple of Christ. It would mean the destruction of the life he had worked so hard to build for himself and his family. Satan's voice whispered in his ear, tempting him with thoughts of unprecedented power and authority.

As he stood before Pilate, Joseph's mind was in turmoil. He could feel the weight of his decision bearing down on him, but he knew that he could not betray his beliefs. So, he offered his assistance to Rome under the pretense to prevent Rome from further trouble with the Jews, hoping to protect himself and his family from the consequences of being associated with a controversial figure like Jesus. He had been tempted by the promises of wealth and power, but in the end, he knew that his loyalty to Jesus and His teachings was worth more than any earthly reward.

Nicodemus, a man of high standing in the Jewish religious community, stepped forward to help with Jesus' burial. His reputation made him a valuable pawn for Satan, who needed him to work with Joseph to confirm the death and burial of Jesus and to take something from the body that Satan can use later. This calculated move was meant to solidify the lie that the disciples had stolen the body, making it the only plausible explanation when the tomb was found empty. But Nicodemus was more than just a respected member of the Sanhedrin party. He was a wealthy and prominent figure, known for his extensive knowledge of the Scriptures. As a cautious Pharisee, he had shown admiration for Jesus but was careful not to be seen with him. This only added to his enigmatic persona. Nicodemus came to Jesus by night, seeking wisdom and answers to his questions. In this encounter, Jesus revealed to him the futility of Pharisaism and the limitations of man-made religion. Despite Nicodemus' status and knowledge, he was just as in need of salvation as anyone else.

Satan cunningly whispered into Nicodemus' ear, luring him with the promise of power and authority. Just like he had tempted Joseph, Satan was now using the same tactic on Nicodemus. And it was working. The thought of being associated with the self-proclaimed Son of God and gaining recognition and influence was too tempting to resist. Nicodemus was already at the top of his field as a religious teacher. He had spent years perfecting his craft, studying and teaching the Scriptures. But there was something about Jesus' teaching that ignited a fire within him. It was as if Jesus had firsthand knowledge of the Scriptures and spoke with a divine authority. Nicodemus couldn't help but be drawn to this young man, whose teachings surpassed his own. Imagine Nicodemus as a senior professor at a prestigious university, with a lifetime of academic achievements and accolades to his name. He had dedicated his entire life to studying and teaching the Scriptures, yet here was this young man, Jesus, who seemed to possess a deeper understanding and command over the Scriptures. Nicodemus couldn't help but feel a mix of admiration, envy, and curiosity towards this remarkable teacher. As he listened to Jesus speak, Nicodemus couldn't help but feel a sense of inadequacy and self-doubt creeping in. How could this young man possess such wisdom and authority? It was like watching a student steal the show from a seasoned professor, leaving Nicodemus questioning his own worth and accomplishments. But despite his inner turmoil, Nicodemus couldn't deny the power and conviction in Jesus' words. There was something undeniable and irresistible about this young man, and Nicodemus was determined to uncover the truth behind his teachings. For the first time in his life, Nicodemus was willing to put aside his pride and reputation in search of a greater understanding.

CHAPTER 8

SIMON HIDES FROM THE EVIL ONE

Alexander's heart pounded in his chest as he watched Simon disappear into the chaotic crowds, the ground beneath them still trembling from the earthquake. Fear and adrenaline coursed through his veins, and he knew this was his only chance to escape the clutches of the Evil One. With determination in his eyes, he pulled his hood over his head, concealing his identity, and weaved his way through the panicked masses. The air was thick with the scent of fear, and the deafening sound of people shouting and pushing filled Simon's ears. He couldn't help but notice the diverse mix of people around him, all caught up in the chaos. There were mothers clutching their children, elderly men struggling to keep up, and young couples desperately trying to hold onto each other. Simon's senses were overwhelmed with the chaos, and he had to fight to keep his mind focused on his goal. Glancing back, he made sure Alexander was safely out of sight before continuing his journey.

The path ahead was treacherous, filled with twists and turns and constantly changing crowds. Simon's mind raced, trying to come up with a plan to get out of the city unnoticed. He knew the Evil One's agents would be searching for him, and he couldn't risk being caught. As he pushed through the crowds, Simon couldn't help but feel a pang of guilt for leaving his son behind. But he knew Alexander would be safer on his own, far away from the chaos and danger. He prayed that his instructions for his son to return to the inn and gather only the essentials would be followed.

However, Alexander had other plans. He couldn't bear the thought of his father facing danger alone, so he secretly followed him from a distance. He stayed hidden, careful not to be spotted by his father, but close enough to keep an eye on him. Alexender's journey was long and treacherous, filled with near misses. He constantly had to change his focus and dodge through the crowds. Every step he took was a risk, and he could feel the weight of the city's chaos bearing down on him. But Alexender was determined to keep an eye out for his father, and for himself. He refused to let the Evil One win. And as he pushed forward, his resolve only grew stronger, fueled by the love for his dad and the desire for their freedom.

The city was in utter chaos, the cries of the people and the clanging of swords filling the air. The darkness of the night provided the perfect cover for Simon's escape, the shadows concealing his every move. His heart raced as he darted through the alleys, his breaths coming in short, panicked gasps. Finally, after what felt like an eternity, Simon reached the city gates. The heavy wooden doors loomed before him, guarded by soldiers with stern, unyielding expressions. But Simon was determined to make it through, to reach the safety of the hill country where his only hope awaited him. He blended in with the incoming and outgoing crowds, disappearing into the darkness like a ghost. His heart hammered in his chest as he passed by the soldiers, praying that they wouldn't notice the sweat on his brow or the tremble in his hands. As he made his way towards the hill country, his mind drifted to his son Alexander and the events of the day. The image of his son's wide, terror-filled eyes as he witnessed the crucifixion burned in his mind. He knew that his son would never be the same after that, and the weight of that knowledge bore down on him like a heavy burden. But he couldn't let himself be consumed by his thoughts. He had to focus on reaching his family, on making it back to them alive.

The path through the hilly country was treacherous, with rocks and uneven terrain threatening to trip him up at every step. But Simon navigated it with ease, his years of experience working outdoors came in handy. The sky above was clear and filled with stars, illuminating his way. It was a stark contrast to the chaos of the city, and for a brief moment, Simon was transported back to a cold winter night from his childhood. He remembered the awe and wonder he felt as he watched the sky light up with a bright light, the stars twinkling like diamonds in the sky, he thought he saw angels dancing through the air and singing. He had asked his father what it meant, and his father had simply replied that he had never seen anything like it before. But now, as he walked towards his family, Simon couldn't help but feel a sense of dread for what was to come. This Passover trip had turned into the darkest day in history, and Simon's only hope was to stay alive and make it back to his loved ones. The night was quiet and peaceful as Simon made his way through the hilly countryside. But inside, his mind was a tumultuous storm of emotions. Fear, guilt, and grief battled for dominance within him, threatening to consume him whole. But he pushed them down, focusing on the task at hand.

As he gazed up at the beautiful lit sky, memories flooded his mind, vivid and intense, as if they were happening all over again. In particular, he remembered the first time he gazed into the eyes of Jesus. The man had a mesmerizing presence, his eyes holding a depth and warmth that drew Simon in. He had never met anyone like him before, and he couldn't help but feel drawn to Him. They were sad and bloodshot yet filled with an indescribable depth and power that captured Simon's soul. In that moment, he experienced pure joy and happiness, and he knew that Jesus was more than just a mere man. He had the power to stop what was happening, but He chose not to. It became clear to Simon that Jesus had a greater purpose, one that required Him to die.

As Simon continues on his journey through the dark hills, his thoughts are suddenly interrupted by the sight of a campfire in the distance. Two figures sit beside it, their faces illuminated by the flickering flames. Simon cautiously approaches, making sure not to alert them to his presence. He passes by unnoticed and continues on, searching for a place to rest for the night. Eventually, he comes across a small cave, bathed in moonlight. It is just big enough for him to sleep in, and he gratefully settles down for the night. As he drifts off into a restless sleep, Simon's mind is plagued by memories of the day's events and the crucifixion. But soon, his exhausted body and mind are pulled into a dream, a dream unlike any he has ever had before. He finds himself standing in front of a blinding light, a light so bright that he can barely keep his eyes open. Yet, as he squints and shields his face, he realizes that he is looking into the eyes of Jesus once again. Intrigued and curious, Simon walks towards the light, feeling a strange pull towards it. As he steps through a door in the back of his mind, he is suddenly transported into another reality. He sees Jesus on the cross, but there is another cross beside Him, and someone is hanging on it too. As he peers closer, he realizes with shock that it is himself, hanging on that cross. And in that moment, Simon understands the true meaning of sacrifice and the depth of Jesus' love for humanity. Jesus' eyes burned with intensity as he gazed at Simon, and his words were like fire in the air. "This day," he said, "you will be with me in Paradise." Simon's confusion and fear only grew as he looked up at the cross, the weight of his own body pressing down on his wrists. "Why am I here?" he cried out, his voice raw with emotion. "What is happening to us?" But Jesus only smiled, a serene and knowing expression on his face. "You will see," he said, his voice ringing with a calm certainty. And see, he did.

As the Roman soldiers around Jesus' cross suddenly transformed into dark, sinister creatures, Simon's heart clenched with terror. He watched as they descended upon him, their claws tearing at his flesh, their voices hissing cruel taunts. "Why, Lord?" Simon screamed, the pain and confusion overwhelming him. But Jesus' voice cut through the chaos, strong and unwavering. "Oh death, where is thy sting?" he declared. "Your life was taken for My name's sake, and your rewards will be great." And then, in a flash of blinding light, Simon's vision shifted. He saw his two sons, grown men now, standing in a church and preaching the word of God. He saw their faith and their devotion, and he knew that he was seeing the future.

But then, just as quickly, his vision changed again. He found himself in a world he didn't recognize, a world filled with chaos and darkness. Simon's soul was taken to a time he could not comprehend, a time far in the future. And there, he saw the world in all its turmoil, as if the gates of hell had been opened. He saw men opening a tomb, and within it lay a body. And he heard their cries of shock and awe: "The body of Jesus has been found!" But this was not the end. He saw Satan's dark angels flying around, worshipping the Evil One and calling him the Antichrist. And in that moment, there were so many of these evil beings that a dense blackness engulfed the tomb, obscuring it from view.

Simon's soul felt lost and alone, surrounded by darkness, so much darkness that it made light feel dead and silent. He longed to feel human again, to escape this endless void. But then, in a burst of light and glory, Jesus appeared in the clouds above. His voice was like thunder, shaking the very foundations of the earth. "Good work, my faithful servant," he said, his eyes shining with pride. "Your work is complete." And with those words, Simon's soul was filled with a sense of peace and purpose. He knew that his sacrifice had not been in vain, that he had played a vital role in the salvation of mankind. And as he basked in the warm light of Jesus' love, he knew that he was truly home, in Paradise. Simon was awestruck by the blinding radiance of Jesus' glory, as he stood surrounded by multitudes of angels that were too numerous to count. It was as if the sun itself paled in comparison to Jesus' brilliance. Simon could feel the heat radiating off of him, and he was sure that if he dared to look directly at Him, he would be blinded. But he couldn't help himself. He had to see, to experience this overwhelming display of power and holiness. As he gazed into the radiant light, Simon's mind was filled with a cacophony of thoughts and emotions.

He was pulled back into reality by the jolt of the morning sun filling the cave where he had slept. For a moment, he was disoriented, unsure of where he was. But then it all came flooding back to him. The dream, or was it a dream? It felt so real, so vivid. Jesus had spoken to him, reassured him that his sons were safe and their lives were blessed. It was a profound experience that left Simon reeling. But now, as he sat in the morning light, the slight breeze blowing in his face, eating the small piece of bread he had stored in his pocket, Simon couldn't shake the feeling that he was being watched. He looked around, but the barren mountain stretched out for miles with no one in sight. Yet, he couldn't shake the feeling that he was not alone. The morning sun was warm, and birds were flying overhead, but something was off. There was an eerie stillness in the air, as if the world was holding its breath. Even the lizards that usually scurried around on the ground seemed to have disappeared. Simon could feel the isolation closing in on him like a suffocating blanket. It was as if a wall had been built around him, trapping him in this desolate place. He knew what was coming. He could feel it in his bones. His time was near, and the future of the church was in jeopardy. Simon didn't understand why, but he knew that he had to be ready to face whatever came his way. Jesus had said, "He who loves his life will lose it, but he who gives up his life for My sake will gain it." Simon knew that in death, he would gain victory in Jesus and ultimately triumph over this dark chapter in his life. As he prepared himself for what was to come, Simon couldn't help but reflect on the complexity of his character. He had worked with his hands outdoors, been a husband, a father, and now a disciple of Jesus. He had faced trials and tribulations, but through it all, he had remained steadfast in his faith. He had come to know Jesus as a powerful and compassionate leader, and he was proud to have served Him. With a heavy heart, but a sense of peace, Simon stepped out of the cave and looked around once more. The emptiness of the mountain mirrored the emptiness in his heart, but he knew that he was not truly alone. Jesus was always with him, and in the end, that was all that mattered.

As the wind howled, a relentless force of nature, Simon shielded his eyes from the stinging sand that whipped across his face. He could taste the grit in his mouth, feel it scratching at his skin. The air was dry and suffocating, making it hard for him to breathe.

But he couldn't look away. He had to see what was coming. His heart pounded in his chest as he strained to make out the shape emerging from the swirling sand. Was it a mirage? A figment of his imagination? No, it was real. And it was coming for him. In that moment, Simon's senses were on high alert. He could hear the sand crunching under the weight of the approaching entity, could smell the musty scent of its breath. Fear gripped him, squeezing his chest and sending shivers down his spine. Who or what was this evil that stalked him in the midst of this barren desert?

Simon's mind raced, trying to make sense of the situation. But all he knew for certain was that he was in grave danger. As the figure drew closer, Simon could make out its twisted features and piercing eyes. It was like nothing he had ever seen before, and yet there was something eerily familiar about it. And in that moment, Simon knew that his fate was in the hands of this mysterious and formidable being. He could only hope that his character and courage would be enough to see him through this encounter.

CHAPTER 9

ALEXANDER FOLLOWS SIMON

Alexander's heart was pounding against his chest as he watched Simon's figure disappear into the sea of people. Fear gripped him, knowing that he had to make a decision. Should he continue following his father, or should he turn back and go to the inn? But he couldn't bear the thought of leaving Simon to face this burden alone. He had to help. With determination, Alexander trailed behind Simon, careful not to be seen. His skills in tracking, acquired through years of hunting, came in handy as he weaved through the crowds. But it wasn't just his physical ability that kept him going. It was the love and admiration he had for his father that fueled his determination. As he followed Simon into the hilly country, Alexander's mind raced with thoughts.

He was proud of his father, and he longed to tell him that. He wanted to give him a hug and go back home, pretending that none of this had ever happened. But he knew that this day would mark his life forever, and this Passover would be remembered for eternity. But who would remember Alexander? He was just the son of Simon from Cyrene, a small and insignificant figure in the grand scheme of things. But as he continued on, he couldn't help but feel that this journey was meant to be. He was meant to be here, following his father, and helping him in any way he could.

Suddenly, Alexander was drawn back to reality by the sight of a glowing campfire. His heart skipped a beat, hoping that it was his father. But he knew that Simon would never build a fire. And as he got closer, he could see two or more silhouettes against the backdrop of the flames. Who were these people? What were they doing here? Questions flooded Alexander's mind as he cautiously approached the campfire. Suddenly, a cold blast of wind swept through the camp, sending shivers down Alexander's spine. As he peered into the darkness, he could see a lurking presence, something unearthly and sinister. His heart pounded in his chest as he remembered his father's warnings about the Evil One coming for him. Could it be true? Could they have already captured Simon? With trembling hands, Alexander crept closer, careful to stay hidden from the inhuman creatures that roamed the camp. He counted four of them, their movements fluid and effortless as they moved in and out of the shadows. What were these things? he wondered, his mind racing with fear and confusion. But before he could make sense of the situation, he stumbled and fell, catching the attention of the creatures. They turned towards him with their glowing red eyes, their razor-sharp fangs glistening in the moonlight. As they stalked towards him, Alexander could feel his heart pounding in his chest, his breaths coming in short gasps. He knew he had made a grave mistake and wished he had followed his father's advice to stay safe at the inn. But to his surprise, the creatures walked right past him, their noses twitching as they searched for their prey. They seemed to have missed him completely, despite looking right at him. It was then that Alexander remembered his father's promise, that Jesus would protect his sons. Was he being shielded from harm? As he lay there, still and silent, Alexander couldn't help but wonder if he was being watched over by angels with flaming swords. The thought filled him with a sense of awe and wonder, despite the danger that still lurked nearby. But he couldn't stay hidden for long.

Exhausted and terrified, Alexander knew he had to find his father and warn him of the danger. He pushed himself up and continued on the path, the moon casting an eerie glow over the rocky terrain.

As he walked, Alexander couldn't shake the feeling that his father had not escaped unnoticed from Jerusalem. He had to find him, and fast. Finally, he came upon a small alcove and crawled underneath to rest. As he looked up at the night sky, he saw the moon, pale and waning, casting a faint light over the landscape. But in that moment, it seemed to shine as bright as the sun, giving Alexander a glimmer of hope. He closed his eyes, exhausted and afraid, and he prayed for morning to come quickly. And as he drifted off to sleep, he couldn't help but wonder what other secrets the night held, and what dangers lay ahead.

CHAPTER 10

JOSEPH BARGAINS FOR JESUS' BODY

As the sky darkened and the cries of agony echoed throughout the land, Jesus hung on the cross, his body battered and broken. Satan watched with malicious glee, knowing that he couldn't tempt Jesus to come down from the cross. But he had another plan, a plan B, the master plan. One that involved using two unsuspecting men: Joseph of Arimathea and Nicodemus, to get something from the body of Jesus that would complete the master plan. Joseph stood at a distance, watching the crucifixion unfold. He was a wealthy man, a member of the Sanhedrin and a friend of Pilate's. But as he gazed upon Jesus, a strange urge overtook him. A desire to get the power of this man who hung before him. It was a thought that penetrated his mind, consuming his every thought. He sent word to Jesus' family, offering to use his own personal tomb to give Jesus a proper burial.

Joseph knew the laws and customs better than anyone, and he knew that a body, especially a Jewish one, couldn't hang on a cross during Passover. If he didn't act quickly, the body would be thrown out for the animals to devour. But this was no ordinary request. By asking for Jesus' body, Joseph was risking his reputation, his status among the high priests and the Sanhedrin. He could be branded a traitor, a sympathizer of this man who had been sentenced to death. But for some reason, Joseph didn't care. Another urge, stronger and more powerful than fear, consumed him. He must get the body of Christ. But why? Where was this desire coming from? As Joseph approached Pilate, he knew he had to be careful. He couldn't reveal his true motives, but he also couldn't lie to his friend. So, he appealed to Pilate's sense of duty to Rome, knowing that it was in their best interest to grant his request.

Meanwhile, Nicodemus, another member of the Sanhedrin, watched with a heavy heart. He had been a secret follower of Jesus, but fear had kept him from publicly supporting him. As he saw Joseph make his way to Pilate, he couldn't help but feel a surge of admiration for this man who was risking everything to honor Jesus in death. Both men were driven by forces they couldn't explain. The crucifixion of Jesus had stirred something deep within them, something that went against everything they had been taught. But as Joseph and Nicodemus laid Jesus' body in the tomb, they knew they had done what was right. They had honored this man who had been unjustly sentenced to death, and they had listened to the voice within them that had urged them to act. It was a voice that would continue to guide them in the days to come, as they grappled with the events of that fateful day on the cross.

Joseph of Arimathea knew that Jesus lacked any formal religious training in the Scriptures, yet His wisdom far surpassed that of the priests. He was in awe of Jesus' ability to perform miracles like healing the sick and raising the dead. The power and authority Jesus possessed was undeniable. Joseph couldn't help but feel a burning desire to have that same power for himself. The thought consumed him, almost assuring him that if he could just touch the body of Jesus, he could receive it. It was a perfect opportunity for him to step up and prove his worth. He convinced himself that if this was truly the Son of God, God would surely reward him for his kindness.

In the midst of this internal struggle, Nicodemus, stepped forward to offer his assistance in burying the body. Nicodemus shared Joseph's belief that Jesus was a man of God and an extraordinary teacher. The two men had been discussing the injustice of Jesus' trial, and when Joseph revealed his plan to request the body, Nicodemus agreed to help. While Joseph went to Pilate's chambers to make his case, Nicodemus gathered burial garments and ointments.

Pilate trusted Joseph and valued his counsel. They had worked together before to resolve Jewish conflicts regarding religious laws. Joseph of Arimathea's shrewd business skills and negotiating abilities were well-known to Pilate. He approached Pilate with caution and respect, knowing that he only had one chance to secure the body of Jesus. He had to make it seem like he was doing a service for Rome and the Jews, or else he risked being disowned by the Sanhedrin and stoned for treason. As he spoke to Pilate, Joseph's voice was rich with determination and purpose. He invoked multiple senses, describing the injustice of Jesus' death and the overwhelming emotions it stirred within him. It was a pivotal moment, and Joseph's actions would have far-reaching consequences. But in that moment, all he could do was hope and pray that he could secure the body of Jesus for a proper burial.

Pilate gestured for Joseph to enter the opulent palace room, overlooking the bustling city below. As he approached, Joseph couldn't help but feel a sense of unease wash over him. He knew the man sitting before him was not to be trifled with. The Roman governor, Pilate, was known for his love of power and his callous disregard for those beneath him. Sipping on a cup of wine, Pilate chuckled as he watched the chaos unfolding in the streets. "You Jews certainly know how to celebrate your religion," he remarked with a sneer, "by killing the one who claims to be your God." Joseph felt a surge of anger rise within him, but he suppressed it, knowing that he needed to tread carefully. As Pilate offered him a cup of wine, they both sat down and engaged in small talk before getting down to business.

Pilate's voice was smooth and calculated as he asked Joseph to explain the nature of his visit. Joseph took a deep breath before speaking. "As you know, Jesus is being crucified as we speak, and at sundown, the Passover starts." Pilate's face darkened, and he interrupted with a dismissive wave of his hand. "I didn't want the poor soul to die. This is your problem to deal with." But Joseph persisted. "I know, and that is why I am here. His family does not have a burial tomb here, and we cannot have the body hanging on the cross during Passover. This could lead to tension within the community and more problems for you. So, I am requesting permission to receive the body and bury Him in my own tomb." Pilate's expression shifted from annoyance to concern. "More problems? What do you mean?" Joseph's voice was laced with urgency as he explained, "So far, Jesus's supporters have not caused any trouble or staged an uprising, but they could be out there right now, plotting. If you disrespect the body by leaving Him hanging on the cross for the birds and wild animals to devour, this could be enough to incite an uprising against Rome. It could cause chaos and destruction in the city, and you know how quickly things can spiral out of control."

Pilate's eyes widened at the thought of a potential revolt. He knew Joseph's words held truth, and he could not risk further unrest in the city. Pilate's face twisted into a scowl as he listened to Joseph's proposal. The stench of fear and desperation hung heavy in the air. The governor's eyes flicked to the guard standing nearby, his hand twitching towards his sword. But then, with a sigh, he lowered his hand and turned back to where Joseph was standing. "I'm trying to do you a favor", continue Joseph, "by taking the body off your hands", Joseph voice laced with frustration. "Rumor has it that Jesus predicted he would rise in three days, and what we believe is that His disciples plan on stealing the body and claiming He came back to life. This would cause the masses to join them in a rebellion against Rome." Joseph's heart pounded in his chest as he watched Pilate's face, searching for any sign of agreement. He knew that his life and the lives of his family were in the balance, depending on the outcome of this conversation. "If I take the body, prepare Him for burial, and then give Him a respectful burial, I can confirm that He is dead and place Him in my tomb where we know there is no back entrance for someone to take the body", Joseph continued. "Plus, we can place guards at the tomb to make sure no one breaks the seal. This will provide you with security and peace of mind." With a resigned sigh, he finally relented. "Fine. Take the body and do as you wish. But make it quick." Pilate summoned one of his guards and gave him strict instructions to report back the moment Jesus was declared dead. He then turned back to Joseph, his eyes narrowing in suspicion.

"What do you want from this then?" Pilate asked, his voice dripping with suspicion. Joseph took a deep breath, his mind racing as he tried to find the right words. He knew that every word he spoke could mean the difference between life and death. "As you know,

I'm a respected leader of the Sanhedrin," he began, his voice steady and confident. "Accordingly, this action on my behalf could put me and my family in danger of other Jewish leaders if they conclude I'm a follower of Jesus, especially after I supported your side of this trial." "My side, questioned Pilate? What do you mean my side?" "I argued against crucifixion and to spare the life of Jesus. So as far as the Sanhedrin, I need for this request to be reported as I'm working on behalf of both Rome and Jerusalem to help defuse this situation before more Jewish citizens get killed." Joseph's heart raced as he spoke, knowing that he was treading on thin ice. But he also knew that this was his only chance to secure a proper burial for Jesus and protect his own family. "Therefore, for security reasons, I was willing to give my tomb on behalf of Jerusalem to secure the body," he finished, holding his breath in anticipation.

Pilate's brow furrowed as he paced back and forth, his mind working through the implications of Joseph's words. Finally, he stopped and turned to face Joseph. "If I'm hearing you right, Jesus claims He would rise from the grave after three days," Pilate said, his voice heavy with disbelief. Joseph nodded, his heart pounding in his chest. This was the moment of truth. He could only hope that Pilate would see the reason in his words and grant his request. "And, I believe this is our only chance to prevent further bloodshed and maintain peace in Jerusalem." Joseph added. Pilate's pacing quickened, the sound of his footsteps echoed off the marble floors, adding to the tension in the room. His thoughts raced as he considered the possible consequences of Jesus' body going missing. The weight of Rome and Jerusalem rested on his shoulders. The conversation with Joseph was filled with underlying tension and suspicion, as both men tried to outmaneuver each other. Pilate's voice was laced with frustration and exasperation as he sat down.

But then, the sudden shaking of the palace and the crashing of artwork created a sense of chaos and urgency. The fear in the room was palpable as they realized it was an earthquake as Joseph fell to the floor. Pilate's command to his servants was sharp and urgent as he commanded them to help Joseph up from the floor, revealing his concern for Joseph's safety. The atmosphere around the table was tense and solemn as they discussed the aftermath of the earthquake, their voices hushed and serious. Just then the officer came to inform Pilate that Jesus was dead. The news of Jesus' death came as a shock to Pilate, his disbelief evident in his question, are you sure?

As Joseph left the palace, he couldn't help but feel a sense of relief and satisfaction. He had succeeded in his mission, and now he could give Jesus the respectful burial he deserved. But he also knew that the tension between the Jews and the Romans was far from over, and he could only hope that his actions would not have any further consequences. Joseph's eagerness to handle Jesus' body was fueled by a mix of curiosity and reverence.

Joseph and Nicodemus' conversation was filled with a sense of urgency and purpose, their voices low and determined. The final exchange between Joseph and Nicodemus revealed a sense of relief and satisfaction, as they had successfully secured permission to bury Jesus' body.

With a sense of urgency, Joseph and Nicodemus retrieve the body of Jesus from the cross. They were both on edge, their eyes darting back and forth as they tried to read each other's thoughts. Joseph knew he needed help, but the presence of another religious leader made him uneasy. Nicodemus, meanwhile, was lost in his own thoughts as he prepared the body to be placed in the donkey drawn cart. The weight of their task hung heavy in the air as they prepared to retrieve the body of Christ.

With the final burial garments left in the tomb, they carefully covered the body and loaded it onto a donkey-drawn wagon. The body seemed to be an unspoken reminder of their own mortality as they made their way to the tomb. The tomb, located in the garden of Gethsemane, was a grand structure with a higher ceiling and a large slab for the body. The solid rock walls seemed to close in on them, adding to the tension in the air. It was a place of finality, and the gravity of the situation was not lost on either man.

As they worked quickly to prepare the body, a mixture of myrrh and aloes filled the air, with their strong scents mingling with the mustiness of the tomb. Joseph and Nicodemus were both lost in their own thoughts, each grappling with the enormity of what they were about to do. As the sun began to set, they knew they had little time left before the Sabbath. Every moment was precious as they made their way to the final resting place of Christ.

CHAPTER 11

SIMON'S DEATH

Simon of Cyrene stood in awe as the valley around him was consumed by a putrid, malicious stench. He knew his fate was sealed, but he prayed for the same courage that Jesus had displayed just days before. This desolate place seemed to be the lair of the Devil himself. As Simon gazed around, he noticed the rugged rocks converging to create what resembled a five-pointed star. Little did he know, this was the very spot where Satan had fallen from grace countless centuries ago. Fear overtook Simon's soul as the malevolence drew nearer. He nervously cracked his knuckles, fully aware that the events at Golgotha were far from over. The black mist approached him, much like the deadly fog that had claimed the firstborns of Egypt during Passover. Simon could only hope for a swift death, similar to those in Egypt. Two dark figures emerged from the mist and circled around him. The stench was unbearable. Soon, more and more figures materialized from the murky edges of the mist until they were innumerable. The mist itself rose up and took the form of a towering creature, standing as tall as the surrounding trees. The creature looked down upon Simon with a wicked laugh, its mouth oozing with a putrid slime. Its forked tongue resembled that of a serpent, while its jagged teeth were as strong as iron, firmly set in its powerful jaws. Its bony hands had long, razor-sharp fingers, and its feet were shaped like those of a goat. Its hollow, fiery eyes bore into Simon, while its large, protruding forehead tapered into a pointed chin. What seemed like horns at first turned out to be a cluster of wuthering snakes, hissing and wriggling in an attempt to break free. As it spoke, fire and smoke emanated from its mouth, accompanied by a rotten stench that shook the ground. Its tail resembled that of a scorpion, ready to strike at any moment.

"Do you claim to be the one who carried the cross and aided Jesus in fulfilling His death mission? I do. You meddled when it was not your place to do so." Satan's voice reverberated, knocking Simon to the ground and paralyzing him with its gaze. Evil surrounded him, but he could only look up from his prone position. "It was my destiny to end Jesus's life, not the cross, not the Romans, but me. And you interfered!" Satan roared. The demons swarmed like locusts during the plagues of Egypt, begging to be unleashed upon Simon, but their master spoke, "In due time, you will have your fill of fun with this one." In a moment, the demon transformed from a towering creature to a human-sized monster. It circled Simon, looking down at him. "What did you see when you looked into Jesus' eyes? Tell me, I know you saw something. What was it?" Simon found his voice and replied, "I saw His glory and your downfall." The creature struck Simon with its tongue, which was more painful than any Roman whip used for flogging. Its sting was more potent than that of a giant scorpion, and blood gushed from the wound. "So, you wish to defy me. Tell me you hate Jesus, and I will release you. Deny Him and curse Him, and you will be set free. There is no need for you to suffer the same death as He did, so just speak the words, and you will go free."

Simon, defiant and resolute, stared up at the demon, refusing to yield. "I will never deny Him. My soul belongs to the Lord, and I will gladly face your wrath rather than betray my savior." The demon's eyes blazed with fury, and it roared with rage, the sound echoing through the valley. "So be it! You will suffer for your insolence! You will know true agony!" With that, the demon unleashed its minions upon Simon. They swarmed him, their touch like fire, their bites like poison. Simon cried out in pain, but his cries were soon drowned out by the sound of his flesh burning and his bones breaking under their assault. Yet, even as his body was torn and battered, his spirit remained steadfast. The demon towered over him, its eyes glowing with a malevolent light. "Still, you defy me? Very well, I will give you one more chance. Denounce Jesus now, and I will end your suffering. Join me, and together, we can rule over this land. It can all be yours." Simon, bloodied and broken, lifted his head, his eyes shining with a light of their own. "I would rather die a thousand deaths than serve you. My loyalty lies with the Lord, and He will be my salvation." The demon's fury knew no bounds, and it raised its bony hands, ready to deliver a fatal blow. Just then, a brilliant light pierced the darkness, causing the demons to shriek and scatter. The light grew stronger, forming a protective barrier around Simon. A figure stepped forward, and Simon recognized him as an angel sent by God. "Your faith has saved you, Simon of Cyrene. Your faith has proven your loyalty, and now you will be rewarded. Rise and join me, for you are destined for greater things." Simon soul, filled with a newfound strength, rose as his body did not. Together, they ascended from the desolate valley, leaving the demon and its minions behind. The battle may have been won, but the war was far from over. Simon, now a warrior of God, knew that his true journey had only just begun.

As Simon's soul and the angel ascended, the demon's furious roars echoed through the valley, a chilling reminder of the evil they were leaving behind. The air grew lighter, and the stench of malevolence faded, replaced by the sweet fragrance of blooming flowers. Simon felt his wounds no longer, his pain easing with each step he took towards the heavens. The angel, a majestic being of radiant light, guided him with a gentle hand. "You have proven your worth, Simon. Your faith in the Lord has not gone unnoticed. Now, a new destiny awaits you." Simon's heart swelled with gratitude and a sense of purpose. He felt empowered, knowing that his act of kindness towards Jesus and his faith in Jesus had not only saved him but also set him on a path of divine service. As they reached the summit of the mountain, a brilliant city came into view. Its streets were paved with gold, and its buildings shone with a celestial light. Simon could hear the harmonious melodies of angels filling the air. "Welcome to the City of God, Simon. A place where the faithful are rewarded and the righteous reign. Your journey has prepared you for what lies ahead." The angel's voice echoed with a soothing resonance. Simon's eyes widened in awe as he beheld the splendor of this heavenly realm. He felt a sense of peace and belonging, knowing that he had left the darkness behind and was now embraced by the light. Beyond the city's gates, a majestic figure awaited them. His presence filled Simon with a profound sense of reverence. "Welcome, Simon of Cyrene," the figure spoke, his voice deep and resonating. "Your courage and faith have not gone unnoticed. You have proven yourself a true warrior of God, and now you shall be rewarded. Enter and take your place among the blessed." Simon, overcome with emotion, fell to his knees. "I am forever grateful, my Lord. My soul is yours, and I am honored to serve." With these words, Simon entered the celestial city, leaving behind the horrors of Golgotha and embracing the eternal glory that awaited him. His journey had come full circle, and he now understood the true meaning of his existence.

CHAPTER 12

ALEXANDER IS PROTECTED

Alexander woke with a jolt, the morning sun blinding him as it streamed in through the cracks of the rocky ledge he had slept under. Instantly, he could feel a prickling sensation on the back of his neck, a sense of danger looming over him. Panic bubbled up in his throat, threatening to choke him. Struggling to breathe, he crawled out from under the ledge and made his way to a small flat rock, collapsing onto it. The world seemed to spin around him as he took in his surroundings. He was in the middle of nowhere, a lone figure in a desolate landscape. The wind howled around him, but he was shielded from its force by a large boulder. He was completely alone. As he sat there, trying to calm his racing heart, Alexander's eyes fell upon a pale brown lizard picking its way along the scabby rocks. He watched it intently, trying to distract himself from the overwhelming sense of doom that hung in the air. He could feel his father's presence nearby, a malevolent force that seemed to seep into every crevice of this desolate place. Alexander knew he had to find his father, to confront him, but he didn't know how close he was. Gathering his courage, he climbed to the top of the hill and peered down the path. And there, in the distance, he saw it. A thick black mist, swirling and pulsating, surrounding an area about three hundred yards away. Alexander's heart sank as he realized his worst fears had come true. His father was surrounded by evil, consumed by it. And he was powerless to stop it. He remembered the words of his dream, the warning from Simon. "There is nothing you can do; this is my destiny now." The words echoed in his mind, taunting him, mocking him. Tears pricked at the corners of Alexander's eyes as he longed to hug his father one last time; to tell him he loved him. How had everything gone so wrong? They were just going to celebrate the Passover, a time of joy and remembrance. But now, it seemed like all hope was lost. As he sat there, lost in his thoughts, Alexander's mind was flooded with memories of the day before. He couldn't make sense of it all. The change that had come over Simon after he looked into the eyes of Jesus. The strange events that followed. It was all too much to bear. But deep down, Alexander knew he couldn't give up. He couldn't abandon his father to this fate. He had to do something, anything. With a determined glint in his eye, he tried to step out from behind the ledge, to make his way towards his father. But something stopped him. A force he couldn't see, but he could feel it holding him back. He tried again and again, but each time, he was pushed back. And then, he heard a soft voice, like a whisper on the wind. "There is nothing you can do. Honor your father and do as he wanted you to do and go home. Take care of the family because God will use you and your brother, Rufus. Don't allow Simon's death to be in vain." The words cut deep into Alexander's heart, reminding him of his duty, his purpose. He knew what he had to do. With a heavy heart, Alexander sat back down on the rock and cried. He cried for his father, for himself, for his family. But most of all, he cried for the loss of innocence, the shattering of his world. And as the tears fell, he made a silent promise to honor his father's memory, to carry on his legacy, and to never forget the lessons he had learned.

As Alexander struggled to his feet, his mind was a whirlwind of fear and confusion. The force that surrounded him, shielding him from the horrors happening just down the way, was blinding him. He tried to see, but all he could make out was the faint outline of his father Simon, writhing in agony. With a deep breath, Alex started walking back towards Jerusalem, determined to figure out what was going on. But as he moved closer, the force grew stronger, pushing him to run. He ran and ran, his heart pounding in his chest, until he couldn't run anymore. Collapsing to the ground, he cried out in frustration and despair. At only twelve years old, Alexander was forced to witness the unimaginable. He was growing up too fast, burdened with the weight of the evil that surrounded him. He knew he could never speak of what he saw, for if the wrong people found out, they would come after him. And if he told anyone, his loved ones would be in danger. As he started the long journey home, Alexander couldn't shake the images from his mind. He vowed to share the story of Jesus, to spread the message of hope and love. But the details of what happened to Simon would stay with him, a secret he would carry to the grave. When he finally arrived home, Alexander knew he would have to explain Simon's absence to his mother and brother. He would have to come up with a story that would ease their worries and give them hope. But deep down, he knew the truth and the truth would haunt him forever. As he prepared to face his family, Alexander couldn't help but wonder if he was growing up too fast, if the weight of this world was too much for a twelve-year-old to bear. But he also knew that in the face of evil, he had to be strong and brave. For the Evil One was everywhere, lurking behind every corner and wall, waiting to pounce on the innocent. But Alexander was determined not to let the darkness win. With a deep breath, he pushed aside his fears and stepped into his home, ready to face whatever came his way.

CHAPTER 13

THE HAIR IS REMOVED

*I gave My back to those who struck Me,
And My cheeks to those who plucked out the beard;
I did not hide My face from shame and spitting.*
—Isaiah 50:6

Joseph and Nicodemus stood in the dimly lit tomb; their eyes fixed on the body of Jesus as they prepared it for burial. Though they were both experts in Jewish law and custom, they could not escape the inner conflict that was raging within them. As they carefully wrapped Jesus' body in layers of fine linen, Joseph couldn't help but think of his own doubts and fears. Despite being a respected member of the Sanhedrin, he couldn't shake the feeling that he was betraying his beliefs by aiding in the burial of this man who claimed to be the Son of God. Nicodemus, on the other hand, was overcome with guilt. He had always been a devout follower of the law, but now he found himself breaking it by helping to give Jesus a proper burial. He knew the consequences could be severe, but he couldn't turn away from the man who had shown him a different way of life. As they worked in silence, their hands expertly applying the burial ointments and spices, their minds were flooded with the prophecies they had learned from the Old Testament. But these prophecies only added to their inner turmoil, as they realized that they were fulfilling the very prophecies that they had once doubted. As they reached Jesus' head, Joseph suggested that they cut off some of his hair as a memento. This idea caused a heated argument between the two men, with Joseph insisting that he deserved to keep more of the hair since he had taken the lead in this burial. Nicodemus, feeling guilty for even being there, reluctantly agreed and even offered a sly comment about gaining powers from the hair. Unbeknownst to them, Satan was lurking in the shadows, pleased with the inner conflict he had caused between the two men. He relished in the fact that Joseph and Nicodemus were going against their morals and beliefs for the sake of this man they barely knew. As they finished their task in the darkness of the tomb, Mary and some of Pilate's guards appeared outside. The guards rolled a large stone across the entrance of the tomb and sealed it with melted wax. Joseph and Nicodemus reassured Mary that everything was taken care of. As they left, the two of them couldn't help but feel a sense of regret for them taking of Jesus' hair. And though they had fulfilled their duty, they couldn't shake the feeling that they had made a grave mistake.

Joseph got home, but before going inside, he turned and looked over one shoulder and then the other. He didn't see anyone, but he could definitely feel someone. He suddenly felt the guilt of a child who told a lie and now must keep the lie from being found out. As he stood there, debating whether to go inside or not, he could hear his wife's voice in his head, reminding him of his promise to always tell the truth. But he couldn't turn back now, not after what he had done. He took a deep breath and opened the door, his heart pounding in his chest. As he entered his house, his wife said, "Good, you're home. It's dinnertime." Joseph forced a smile and kissed his wife on the cheek, trying to act normal. But inside, he was panicking. What if someone had seen him at the burial site? What if they knew what he had done? He marched directly to the back of his house to hide the hair before he went to dinner, and he just hoped his wife or family didn't notice the bag he was carrying. But as he sat down at the dinner table, he couldn't shake off the feeling of being watched. He was quieter than normal, lost in his thoughts and consumed by guilt. His wife noticed his behavior and asked him if he was all right. Joseph stalled the conversation for a few minutes, trying to come up with a believable story. But his wife could see through his lies and asked him directly about the burial. Joseph's heart raced as he tried to come up with a way to explain without revealing his secret. He realized he was being evasive and then went into considerable detail of how things unfolded and how the burial went, leaving out the part about the hair. But as he spoke, his conscience weighed heavily on him. He couldn't believe he was lying to his own wife, the person he loved most in the world. As the night wore on, Joseph was edgy and continued to feel like his home was being watched. He couldn't sleep, tossing and turning in bed as his mind raced with thoughts of his deception. He finally turned in, hoping that a night of sleep would clear his head, and that tomorrow would be a new day without this feeling. But even in his dreams, he couldn't escape the guilt and fear that consumed him. He drifted off to sleep, only to be plagued by a dark dream. He was falling through darkness, and then without warning, he was running down a narrow winding path lined with barren trees. Branches were hanging down so low they hit him in the face as he ran through them. He felt a sense of dread and knew he was being chased. He saw a broken-down gate in front of him. Joseph didn't want to go through it because he knew there would be no return, but he had no other choice. Faceless priests and religious leaders were chasing him, trying to get their hands on the hair of Jesus. They held stones in their hands, and if they caught him, he would be killed. As he was running, he looked behind him, and no one was chasing him anymore. He was in a dark, cold cave underground, and he could feel evil all around him. Then an old man with dirty, raggedy clothes emerged from the darkness with a torch that lit the room. Reflections of the shadows were bouncing off the ceiling. "You have something that is mine, give it to me," he demanded, his voice echoing through the cave. "What do I have that is yours, old man?" Joseph said, trying to keep his composure. "The hair. It is mine—and here is what you need to do," the old man said, his eyes burning with anger. Joseph's heart sank as he realized the truth. The old man was the true owner of the hair, and by taking it, Joseph had placed himself in danger. The old Man told Joseph to take the hair the next morning to and old beggar who will be setting at the corner down the street. He was torn between his fear of the old man and his guilt for betraying his beliefs. But in the end, his fear won, and he gave in to the Old Man's demands. As he woke up, drenched in sweat, Joseph realized the true cost of his actions. He had not only betrayed his beliefs but also put himself in danger.

As Joseph sat on the edge of his bed, his mind raced with conflicting thoughts. He couldn't shake the feeling that something was off, that this wasn't just a mere nightmare. But at the same time, he couldn't bring himself to believe that Satan had actually visited him. In a moment of panic, Joseph got up and stumbled to the window, his heart racing as he peered out into the darkness. For a split second, he thought he saw a figure standing outside his house, but when he blinked, it was gone. He shook his head, trying to clear his mind of the disturbing image. But as he turned to go back to bed, a foul stench assaulted his nostrils, causing him to gag. He frantically searched the room, trying to find the source of the smell, but there was nothing. Just as he was about to dismiss it as a figment of his imagination, a voice whispered in his ear, "I've been waiting for you, Joseph." Joseph's blood ran cold as he spun around, but the room was empty. He knew he needed to do something, but he couldn't bring himself to move. Fear rooted him to the spot as he waited for the next sign of the demonic presence.

The next morning, Joseph woke up early, his mind still reeling from the events of the previous night. He couldn't shake the feeling that he needed to do something, but he didn't know what. As he got dressed, he couldn't help but think that he was being watched, that the evil presence was still lingering around him. But as he stepped outside, he was met with the sight of a raggedy old man with dark, hollow eyes. In an instant, the man transformed into a creature straight out of his nightmares. Joseph's heart raced as he stumbled back into his house, slamming the door shut behind him. He knew he needed to do something, but the thought of facing such a powerful evil made him want to run and hide. He was just a simple man, what could he possibly do against Satan himself? But then he remembered the dream he had before all of this started. The dream where a voice had told him what he needed to do. It went against everything he believed in, but he knew it was the only way to defeat the evil that had invaded his life. With a heavy heart, Joseph made his way out of the house, a hidden object clutched tightly in his hand. As he walked down the street, he could feel the weight of centuries-old spirits all around him, their whispers echoing in his mind. He wanted to turn back, to forget about this whole ordeal, but he knew he couldn't. He had to see this through to the end, no matter the cost.

EVIL DECEPTION

Without warning, the temperature dropped ten degrees, and the stench stopped Joseph in his tracks. He shivered and wrapped his arms around himself, feeling a sense of unease wash over him. He knew he wasn't alone, but he couldn't see anyone around. His heart raced as he continued to walk, the feeling of being watched creeping up his spine. He tried to push the thoughts away and focused on his mission to find the beggar. But as he got closer to the corner, his mind started to race with doubts and fears. What if the beggar was just a decoy? What if he was walking into a trap? Joseph's hand instinctively reached for his hidden weapon, but he hesitated. He couldn't bring himself to harm someone in need, no matter how suspicious the situation seemed. As he stopped to catch his breath, Joseph's mind was in turmoil. He knew he should turn and run, but he also knew he must confront the beggar. He closed his eyes and took a deep breath, trying to calm his racing thoughts. But just as he opened his eyes, he saw the beggar's face. He recoiled in horror at the sight of the beggar's twisted, scarred features. A chill ran down his spine as the beggar's hollow eyes seemed to stare right through him. Joseph's hand shook as he reached into his coat, knowing what he had to do. He pulled out the hair, feeling a surge of guilt and shame came over him. He had betrayed his own beliefs, his own values, all for the sake of his mission. He handed the hair to the creature, unable to meet its gaze. He had stared into the eyes of evil and had been used by it. As he quickly tried to leave the area, Joseph couldn't help but look back one last time. The beggar was nowhere to be seen, but Joseph couldn't shake off the feeling of being watched. He quickened his pace, feeling relieved to be away from the beggar, but also feeling a heavy weight on his chest. He knew he had done something unforgivable. As he walked down the street, Joseph's mind was filled with questions and doubts. What did Satan want with Jesus' hair? What did he plan to do with it?

And most importantly, how had he let himself be a part of this evil plan? The guilt ate away at him, gnawing at his conscience. He had betrayed not only the world, but also Jesus himself.

Meanwhile, across town, Marcus, the Roman soldier who had Jesus' robe, was facing his own danger. Marcus was an early riser, known for his strong sense of duty and discipline. He prided himself on his ability to remain calm and collected in any situation. But as he sat alone in his room, his mind was consumed by conflicting thoughts and emotions. He couldn't shake the memory of yesterday's events, when he had witnessed the crucifixion of Jesus. The man's claims of being the Son of God had been met with ridicule and disdain from many, including Marcus. He had laughed along with the others, relishing in the misguided Jew's suffering. But as he replayed the scene in his mind, Marcus couldn't help but feel a twinge of guilt. Was he wrong to mock someone's beliefs? Was it truly right to take pleasure in someone's pain? These thoughts troubled him, but he pushed them aside, reminding himself that he was a soldier, a loyal servant of the Roman Empire. Just as he was trying to silence his inner turmoil, a deep chill washed over him, followed by a nauseating stench of death. Marcus felt a shiver run down his spine and his heart began to race. He looked around the room, trying to find the source of the disturbance. But there was nothing. Just an empty room with closed windows and locked doors. Marcus couldn't understand what was happening, but a sense of dread began to fill him. Evil seemed to seep into the room, suffocating him with its presence. For the first time in his life, Marcus felt fear. It was a foreign and unsettling feeling that he couldn't control. His mind raced with questions and doubts, and he couldn't find any answers. Suddenly, a voice cut through the silence, causing Marcus to jump. "You stupid fool," the voice said, echoing around the room. Marcus's hand instinctively reached for his sword, but there was no one there. "You have no idea who wore that robe," the voice continued, "and yet you sit here and gloat and laugh about some misguided Jew. Even the demons know that Jesus is the Son of God." Marcus's heart dropped as he realized the truth of the words. He had been blinded by his own pride and prejudice, unable to see the truth that was right in front of him. He had made a grave mistake, and now he was facing the consequences. "Show yourself," Marcus demanded, his voice trembling with fear and anger. But the voice only laughed, taunting him with his own foolishness. And in that moment, Marcus knew that he had failed. He had failed as a soldier, as a human being, and as a man. The weight of his actions and choices crashed down on him, and he knew that he would never be able to escape the guilt and regret that now consumed him.

"What do you think you're doing?" growled the voice, its intensity causing shivers to run down his spine. "Do you honestly believe I will allow you to take me like Jesus did?" A deep, ancient wisdom, far beyond his own, drew his attention to the robe. As he gazed upon it, he could feel its power emanating from every thread, a brilliant light that surrounded it and then vanished. But he was not alone. The room was filled with an unseen force, one that snatched the robe away from him. Suddenly, two silhouettes materialized, and he was transfixed, unable to move as they floated around him. They were unlike anything he had ever seen. Their forms were both terrifying and mesmerizing, their presence overwhelming. He wanted to run, to escape their grasp, but his body refused to obey. As they passed through him like wisps of smoke, a chill unlike any other gripped him, sending a rush of fear and awe through his veins. This was no ordinary encounter, and he knew he was in the presence of something far greater, far more complex than he could ever imagine. But who were these beings? What did they want from him? And what was the true power of the robe that had drawn them here? Marcus looked at them, and he saw his fate: a bloody pile of fleshy bones was lying on the floor, like a lion had torn a body apart. He knew it was his own body.

"What do you want?" asked Marcus.

Without a word, the demon sliced Marcus's head off his shoulders, and it hit the floor before his knees even buckled. The other demon cut him up into a mangled mess. "Nothing, nothing at all...except maybe your head and the robe," answered the demons. The demons took the robe and Marcus' head back to Satan. They flew through the murky depths of the underworld, their wings beating against the thick, suffocating air. The stench of sulfur and decay filled their nostrils as they descended deeper and deeper into the dark abyss. Lucifer's lair awaited them, and they could feel his powerful presence beckoning them forward. Summoned by the devil himself, they entered the chamber and immediately dropped to their knees, bowing before their dark master.

The chamber was a sight to behold - protected by fierce beasts and twisted creatures, the walls glowed with an eerie, pulsating light that seemed to emanate from the very depths of hell. Satan sat upon a towering throne made of the tortured souls of those who had defied him. His eyes, burning with a fierce intensity, scanned the two demons as they approached him. In their hands, they carried a robe, the robe of Jesus, the Son of God. With a cruel laugh, Satan snatched the robe from their grasp and draped it over his broad, muscular shoulders. "So, this is the garment of the Son of God," he sneered. "We will see just how much faith the world has in him when I present his dead body to them." With the robe, Satan now had all the pieces he needed to carry out his twisted Master plan. The hair of Jesus, the blood-stained crown of thorns, and now the robe, all infused with the power of DNA, a concept he had mastered in his centuries of existence. As Satan reveled in his triumph, he knew that his master plan would bring about the downfall of the arrogant and unbelieving world, he could not help but feel a sense of admiration for his cunning and complex scheme. For in his twisted mind, Satan was not just a mere devil, he was a mastermind, a manipulator, a force to be reckoned with. And as he plotted the downfall of humanity, he could not help but feel a sense of shock and awe at the concept of such a scheme.

CHAPTER 14

SATAN RETURNS TO THE TOMB

Satan's presence loomed over Simon's tomb, his black cloak billowing in the wind as he descended from the sky. A deafening roar echoed through the air, as if the very earth was trembling in fear. The ground shook violently as Satan's feet touched down, sending clouds of dust and debris swirling into the air. The sky darkened, as if the very heavens were weeping at the sight of the devil's arrival. With a sinister grin, Satan surveyed the scene below him. He had been waiting for this moment, planning and plotting for centuries. And now, it was finally within his grasp. The final pieces of his master plan were about to fall into place, and nothing would stand in his way. As he gazed down at the tomb, his mind raced back to the beginning of time. He remembered the day when God had announced his plan to create man and establish a new covenant. A covenant that would elevate man above the angels, a thought that filled Satan with rage and jealousy. How dare God place these mere mortals above him and his fellow angels? In that moment, Satan's betrayal and anger had consumed him. He had tried to overthrow God, accusing him of not knowing what he was doing. But in the end, he and his followers were cast out of heaven, banished to a life of eternal damnation. And now, he was determined to take his revenge. Satan's army of fallen angels stood by his side, ready to do his bidding. They knew the stakes were high, for this battle would determine the fate of their existence. But Satan was confident that he would emerge victorious, and his crushing blow would be felt around the world. As he prepared to carry out his plan, Satan's voice was filled with malice and determination. He was a complex and intriguing character, with a burning hatred for God and a desire for power and glory. And as he unleashed his wrath upon the world, he evoked strong emotions of fear and despair in all who witnessed his presence. For Satan was the epitome of evil, and his reign of terror would be felt for eternity.

Man had been a thorn in Satan's side ever since, and Jesus was determined to protect humanity—even to the point of becoming human and dying. Satan could never figure that one out. What did God have to gain by protecting the weak, foolish human race? Yet, here Jesus was, sacrificing himself for them. It was a concept that baffled Satan, yet he couldn't help but admire the sheer audacity of it all. As he stood over the body of Simon, Satan couldn't help but feel a twinge of envy. The man had been chosen to play the role of Jesus in Satan's grand plan. And what a role it was. Simon's body, now lifeless, lay in a tomb that Satan himself had designed. It was a masterpiece, a monument to his cunning and power. Satan's eyes scanned the engraved names of the disciples on the stone walls. He had made sure to include pledges for them to continue the religion in the name of their fallen leader. It was all part of his plan to deceive and manipulate the weak-minded humans. But as Satan looked down at Simon's body, he couldn't help but feel a tinge of regret. The man had been a loyal follower, and now he was being used as a pawn in Satan's game. But then again, that was the way of the world. The strong preyed on the weak, and Satan was the strongest of them all. With a wicked grin spreading across his face, Satan examined the wounds on Simon's body. They were exactly as Jesus'—the crown of thorns, the nail holes in the wrists and feet, and the wound to the side. It was crucial for everything to appear genuine, to pull off his ultimate deception. The humans were nothing but pawns in his grand game, and he would stop at nothing to win. And with that thought, Satan laughed, a deep, sinister laugh that echoed through the tomb. Simon may have made a splendid Jesus, but Satan was the mastermind behind it all. He was the one pulling the strings, and he would continue to do so until the end of time. After Satan examined Simon's bloodied corpse, he viciously barked orders at his demons to prepare the body according to Jewish custom.

The stench of death and decay filled the air as the demons scrambled to follow his commands, using the proper burial techniques, clothing, and spices. It was a sight that would make even the bravest of warrior's tremble in fear. Joseph and Nicodemus, two devout and meticulous men, had meticulously followed every detail of the Jewish custom when preparing Jesus for burial. Satan, being the cunning and meticulous being that he was, oversaw the wrapping of Simon's body, making sure it was done exactly as written. But he couldn't resist making a few changes. With a wicked grin, he removed Simon's hair and replaced it with that of Jesus', knowing that hair can survive for thousands of years and provide DNA evidence. He then carefully placed the crown of thorns on the slab next to the corpse, fully aware of the archaeological significance it would hold. But Satan's devious plan didn't end there. He meticulously folded the robe and placed it in the corner of the room, on a ledge where it would be easily found. He knew that the Bible would record that the Roman soldier got the robe, but what it wouldn't mention, is the DNA evidence that would prove this body to be that of Jesus. Satan couldn't help but revel in his own cunning and deceitfulness. He knew that once the body was found, and DNA testing declared it to be Jesus', the Bible would no longer be considered trustworthy. All the evidence, including the robe, would point to Jesus being dead.

As he looked down at Simon's lifeless body, Satan couldn't help but think, "At least you will receive a proper burial, Simon." A small satisfaction amidst all the chaos and destruction he had caused. He knew that when the tomb was discovered, scholars would flock to examine the remains for authenticity. And he wanted everything to be perfect, to ensure that his devious plan would come to fruition. This was Satan at his most cunning and conniving, using every trick in his arsenal to deceive and manipulate. And deep down, a part of him relished in the chaos and destruction he had caused. Because that's who he was, the ultimate deceiver, always one step ahead, and always relishing in the downfall of others.

CHAPTER 15

ALEX'S JOURNEY HOME

Alexander was lying in bed filled with uncertainty about his future. Lost in his sleep and dreams, when he found himself floating outside of reality, revisiting memories from his childhood. He saw himself as a carefree child, playing with his brother Rufus under the watchful eyes of his parents. The sun was shining, and his parents were laughing and chasing after them, but then things took a strange turn. He transformed into a butterfly and flew away, questioning why this change had occurred. As he flew back towards his family, he saw Rufus and his mother crying and beckoning for him to return, but his father Simon was nowhere to be found. Despite the temptation to keep flying away, he knew he had to return to his family and transform back into Alexander. Suddenly, he jolted awake in bed, momentarily disoriented and ready to run. He frantically looked around for answers before realizing he was back at the inn where he and his father had stayed upon their arrival. It felt like a distant memory now, even though it had only been a short time ago. With a long journey ahead of him, Alexander washed his face and gathered his belongings to prepare for the day. As he stepped outside into the dark morning, the cold air jolted him awake as if reminding him that it was a new day with new opportunities. Taking a moment to collect himself, he planned his route home and set off on his journey.

He had been trudging along the trail for what felt like an eternity, the weight of his father's death heavy on his shoulders. The crisp morning air burned in his lungs as he pushed through the barren landscape, his feet aching and his stomach growling. But then, the sunrise stopped him dead in his tracks. A blinding red disk appeared in the sky, its brilliance casting a spell over the desolate landscape. It was as if the world had been holding its breath, waiting for this magnificent display of light and color. Alex couldn't tear his eyes away as the sun grew into a massive ball of fire, shedding its dark orange for a fiery yellow as it announced its presence in the sky. He couldn't help but marvel at the beauty of it all, this reoccurring miracle of the morning sunrise. But as the sun continued its journey across the sky, Alex couldn't shake the weight of his thoughts. How could the earth not know that Jesus, one claiming to be her God, and his own father Simon had just been brutally killed? As he continued on his journey, Alex remained cautious and alert, wary of every person he encountered. He knew that as a twelve-year-old boy, it would be safer to travel with others, but he just wasn't ready to open up and trust anyone yet. As the day gave way to the vibrant hues of sunset and then the enveloping darkness of nightfall, Alex searched for a dry spot to bed down for the night. The darkness seemed thicker than usual, and he was grateful for the small fire he managed to start. As he cooked a simple meal, the crackling of the flames and the smell of the food brought a small sense of comfort. But that comfort was shattered when two strangers suddenly appeared behind him, startling him out of his thoughts. He couldn't help but feel a sense of unease, his instincts telling him to be cautious and on guard. Who were these strangers, and what did they want? Alex couldn't help but wonder as he cautiously watched their every move. "Quite a young one to be wandering all alone," one of the strangers remarked, his voice dripping with suspicion. His companion, a gruff and rough-looking man, rifled through Alex's belongings without a care in the world. Alex stiffened, his heart pounding in his chest. He knew he was too young to be traveling alone, He didn't think it would be a problem, but now these strangers were making him doubt his decision. "My father went down the trail to get some herbs. He'll be back any moment," Alex said, trying to sound confident. "So, you should leave now." The man who had been searching through his food pack snorted. "Not so fast, little one. You're traveling alone, aren't you?" He grabbed a handful of Alex's food and began stuffing it into his own pack. "Stop! You can't do that, it's mine!" Alex protested, his voice rising in desperation. "When my father gets back, he'll show you." The other stranger smirked, his eyes glinting with greed. "A fine, young lad like you could fetch a good price for the right buyer." Just then, three men appeared out of thin air, surrounding the strangers. Alex's heart skipped a beat as he realized they were not ordinary men, but something more. "Did you hear the boy? You need to leave now and put all that food back," one of the men said, his voice firm and commanding. The strangers, taken aback by the sudden appearance of the three men, stumbled over themselves as they hurried to leave. Alex stared at them in awe, his fear momentarily forgotten. He couldn't believe what he was seeing. Who were these men? And how did they make those strangers flee so easily? "Thanks, but I'll be fine on my own," Alex said, his voice shaking slightly. "We know you will be fine, but if you don't mind, we'll travel with you. We're going in the same direction," one of the men said, a warm smile on his face. Alex felt a sense of peace wash over him as he looked at the three men. He knew they were here to protect him, and he felt grateful for their presence. "I'm Elijah, and these are my friends, Daniel and Michael," the man introduced himself and his companions. "I'm Alex," he replied, feeling a sense of relief wash over him.

"We know." The words hung heavy in the air, carrying a weight of knowledge and understanding. Alexander, the son of Simon from Cyrene, sat by the fire, his eyes locked on the dancing flames. His mind was a whirlwind of questions, sorrow, and anger. His father had died for a man he had known only through stories. But who? And why? Elijah, a man with a weathered face and eyes full of wisdom, spoke again. "You are safe with us, Alexander. We will answer all your questions in due time. But for now, rest." Alex turned to face the man, his expression filled with confusion and frustration. "Why should I trust you? Who are you to care about me?" Elijah's gaze softened. "In the morning, Alexander. In the morning." The next day dawned, but Alexander had slept through it. He opened his eyes to find the sun high in the sky, and his companions deep in conversation. Elijah and Daniel, a man with a quiet strength, were engaged in a heated debate. Michael, a quiet and observant man, stood watch over the campsite. Alexander sat up, rubbing the sleep from his eyes. "What time is it?" "Almost noon of the second day," Daniel replied. "Second day?" Alex's voice rose in shock. "What happened to the first day?" Michael gave a small smile. "You slept through it, with a little help from Elijah. He thought you needed the rest."

Alexander stood, his body ready for answers, but Elijah wasn't ready to give them yet. "You will have your answers, Alexander. But first, you must eat and regain your strength." As they ate, Elijah began to tell Alexander the truth about his father, about Rufus, and about his own role in their journey. And with each word, Alexander's understanding and perspective shifted. He no longer saw Elijah as a stranger, but as a mentor and a friend. As the day wore on, Alexander's mind and heart were opened to new experiences and new emotions. And as night fell once again, he knew that this journey would change him in ways he couldn't even imagine. "Patience, my little friend," Elijah's voice was stern yet gentle, "there is plenty of time for answers, but right now we must get you some food so we can get on the road." The urgency in his tone was palpable as he looked at Alexander with a serious expression.

Daniel rummaged through Alex's stash of food, searching for something that would satisfy their hunger. But as he looked through the meager supplies, he couldn't find anything that would do. He glanced over at Alexander, who seemed to be watching him closely, and then turned to an empty sack. With a quick movement, he pulled out a plate full of food and brought it over to Alexander. The boy's eyes widened in surprise as he looked at the plate. "Where did you get this food?" he asked, his curiosity piqued. Daniel just smiled mischievously and replied, "I cooked it up myself." He then returned to sit by Elijah, who had remained silent throughout the exchange. As Alexander finished his meal and gathered his things, the four of them set out for home. Alexander walked beside Elijah, hoping to engage him in conversation about Simon. But Elijah remained quiet, testing the young boy's patience. After two hours of walking, Alexander suddenly veered off the trail and sat down under a low-hanging tree branch. Elijah, Daniel, and Michael stopped and looked at him, and Michael asked, "Are you tired?" "No," Alexander replied, his tone determined. Sensing that Alexander needed some answers, Elijah told Daniel and Michael that he would take care of it. He walked over to Alexander and sat down next to him. "All right

Alex," he began, "you deserve to know the truth. But I must warn you, it may be difficult for you to understand and accept."

Alexander said, "Then tell me only fragments, small bits of information, so I can piece it together myself. Alexander's words cut through the air like a sharp blade. Start with who Daniel, Michael and you truly are." As they spoke, Alexander was transported to a surreal world, a dreamlike landscape where Elijah, Daniel, and Michael stood by his side. "What do you see?" Elijah's voice echoed in the vast space. "I see a staircase of dazzling lights, stretching up into the sky and beyond the clouds. It leads all the way to heaven," Alexander replied, his eyes wide with wonder. Elijah pressed on, "And where are you now, Alexander?" "I'm standing on a grand platform, surrounded by a sea of people dressed in shimmering white robes. I see you, Daniel, and Michael, but Michael's appearance is unlike anything I've ever seen. Everyone here glows with an otherworldly radiance. And there, at the center of it all, I see a figure shining like the sun, and all are bowing down to Him." Elijah's words resonated with a deep sense of truth and understanding. "Daniel and I are souls from the past, prophets of God who once walked this very earth, just like you and your father Simon. And Michael, he is an archangel from heaven, a powerful protector sent to safeguard your true identity from the clutches of Satan. And that glowing figure, that is Jesus, the very same one your father Simon helped carry His cross. Now, look down to earth and tell me what you see, Alexander." Alexander peered over the edge of the platform, his heart racing with anticipation. And there, far below, was a young boy working alongside his father in a humble wood shop. The boy's mother called out, "Jesus, it's time for lunch." The boy said goodbye to his father and bounded towards the house. As he walked, he noticed a small, lifeless bird lying on the ground. Without hesitation, he scooped it up and held it in his hands. Tears streamed down his face as he whispered to the bird, "Please, my friend, fly again." And to everyone's amazement, the bird came back to life and soared into the sky. Alexander listened as the boy's father explained the concept of death, and the boy's innocent response brought tears to his eyes. "But that was my friend," he said, his voice filled with pure and unadulterated love. Through his tears, Alexander heard the father caution his son not to use his powers recklessly. And the boy replied, "Yes, Father, but that was my friend." And in that moment, Alexander realized the profound depth of love and compassion that existed in this world, a love that could even conquer death itself.

"Then Elijah's voice grew grave and intense, his eyes blazing with fervor. 'That young Jesus,' he declared, 'is the very same Jesus who died on the cross for our sins. He is God incarnate, the one who shines with divine radiance and deserves all our worship.' With a commanding gesture, he turned to the others and asked, 'Tell me, what do you see now?' Alexander trembled, his eyes wide with fear. 'I see darkness,' he whispered, 'evil everywhere. Babies being slaughtered, the human race spiraling out of control. And those creatures, like the ones I saw around my father, scouring the earth for something.' Elijah's voice was filled with righteous anger as he explained, 'What you are witnessing is the work of Satan, trying to kill the baby Jesus. He has corrupted the hearts and minds of humanity, leading them away from God the Creator. He wanted to destroy God's own creation, believing that if he could corrupt all of humankind, there would be no one worthy enough to give birth to the promised savior. But God had a plan, and the Savior was born despite Satan's efforts. He hid the identity of baby Jesus from the devil, allowing him to grow up in peace.' Alex's heart raced as he listened, his emotions in turmoil. 'But why did we see those evil beings searching for the child?' he asked, his voice trembling. Elijah's expression softened. 'Because Satan never gives up,' he replied. 'He knows that the Savior is the only hope for humanity, and he will stop at nothing to try and destroy him. But God is always one step ahead, and He will protect His son until the time is right.'

As Elijah's words sank in, Alexander eyes filled with both fear and hope. He now understood the magnitude of the battle between good and evil and knew that the fate of the world rested on the shoulders of a young boy. But he also knew that with God on their side, there was still a chance for redemption. 'What do you see now?' Elijah asked once more, his voice filled with determination. Alex's gaze swept across the room; his senses heightened by Elijah's words. And for the first time, he saw a glimmer of light amidst the darkness, a spark of hope in the midst of despair. 'I see a child,' he answered, his voice strong. 'A child who will one day save us all.' Elijah smiled, his eyes shining with pride. 'Yes,' he said, 'that is exactly what we see too.' And in that moment, Alexander knew that he would follow the young Jesus, no matter where their journey took them, for he had seen the truth, and his heart was forever changed."

"What do you see now?" asked Elijah!

"I see a battle where a lion viciously attacks a lamb. The lion circles the lamb as it is lying there bloody and lifeless, but then the lamb's shepherd appears from nowhere and with one swing of His staff, He slices the lion's throat open and stands on the dying carcass in victory. "The meaning behind that," Elijah's voice grew intense as he spoke, "involves the cross, the crucifixion of Jesus', and His resurrection. You and Simon saw Jesus die on the cross, but what you didn't see was that Jesus came back to life again after three days.

Can you imagine the power of that moment? The overwhelming joy and awe as Jesus rose from the dead, defeating death itself. It's a miracle that continues to give hope and strength to believers all over the world." Elijah's words hung in the air, the weight of their significance sinking in. But as he continued, the atmosphere shifted, becoming charged with a sense of urgency. "There is a holy war that started millions of years ago when Satan, an archangel on the same order as Michael, rebelled against God and all that God created. His pride and desire for power led him to try and overthrow God, but he was cast out of heaven and onto the earth. And when God created man, Satan saw an opportunity to corrupt and destroy God's creation. But God had a plan to defeat Satan once and for all." Elijah's voice took on a somber tone as he spoke of the ongoing battle between good and evil. "God promised that a savior would come, a promised seed, to defeat Satan and redeem humanity. Satan tried to stop Jesus from fulfilling his destiny by tempting him and even attempting to kill him as a child. But Jesus prevailed and grew into a man, ready to fulfill his purpose on earth." "As you know, Simon played a crucial role in Jesus' death. He helped Jesus carry his cross and reach Calvary, where he was ultimately crucified. Simon's actions were essential for the salvation of all humanity by helping Jesus to the cross. In that moment, he became a figure of immense significance in history." Elijah paused, his eyes searching mine as he continued. "But Satan was not pleased. He saw Simon as a threat, a key player in God's plan to defeat him. And so, he set his sights on Simon, seeking to destroy him and use his body for his own devious purposes, to counterfeit the very death of Jesus. But Simon's sacrifice and bravery were not in vain." A shiver ran through Alexander as he listened to Elijah's words. The weight of the spiritual warfare happening behind the scenes was almost too much to comprehend. "But Satan is not finished yet," Elijah's voice grew even more intense, "he has one final plan to deceive the world and lead them astray. And Simon's body is at the center of it all. He will present Simon's body as the body of Jesus, and the world will be deceived. But do not fear, my child. For Michael, the archangel, and two prophets of God are here on earth, standing in the way of Satan's plan. And together, with the power of God on our side, we will defeat him." Elijah's words filled me with a sense of determination and courage. The battle was far from over, but I knew that with God's help, we could overcome any obstacle. "Satan is coming, my friend," Elijah's eyes blazed with determination, "but so are we. And we will not let him win."

CHAPTER 16

BATTLE ON EARTH

Unrest stirred in the depths of the underworld, and the earth shook with fear. The very ground trembled beneath the weight of Satan's agitation. His plan to deceive the world was flawless, but something was wrong; something was out of place. The air was thick with whispers of trouble, carried on the lips of the wind. Satan could feel it, a sense of unease, a presence that he couldn't quite place. He knew he had missed something, and it gnawed at him like a festering wound. "I will not be outsmarted," he growled, his voice echoing through the caverns of hell. "This is my earth, and nothing shall go on here that I do not know about." With a flick of his hand, he summoned his army of demons, ready to carry out his orders. But then, a presence unlike any other made itself known. A powerful, heavenly presence that sent a shiver down Satan's spine. It was the archangel Michael, a formidable foe and a spirit that Satan knew all too well.

They had battled before, in the very halls of heaven, and Satan knew that this would be no different. As he paced back and forth, plotting his next move, Satan could feel Michael's energy growing stronger. He knew that the archangel was preparing for battle, and Satan couldn't help but feel a sense of unease. Michael was a mighty warrior, an archangel like no other commanded a massive army of angels, and his power far exceeded that of any other heavenly being, except one: Lucifer, also known as Satan. But Michael had something that Satan did not, the radiant glow of Jesus' glory, and the authority to command the heavenly hosts. As he prepared for battle, his wings burst forth from his shoulder blades with a twelve-foot wingspan, and his sword began to glow with an otherworldly light. The tension in the air was palpable as the two forces readied themselves for battle.

As Michael's presence transformed into that of a fully battle-ready commander, he couldn't help but think back to the battle that started it all. It was a battle that had been recorded in history, a battle that changed everything. "And war broke out in heaven: Michael and his angels fought with the dragon; and the dragon and his angels fought, but they did not prevail, nor was a place found for them in heaven any longer." The words echoed in Michael's mind as he prepared to face his old adversary once again. But this time, the battle would be on earth, and the stakes were higher than ever before. The mere thought of facing Michael in battle sent a surge of adrenaline through Satan's body. He knew that this would be a battle unlike any other, a battle that would test his strength and cunning ability. But he was ready. He would not let Michael or anyone else stand in the way of his plans. As the two forces clashed, the very earth trembled beneath their feet. And as the battle reached its climax, it was clear that only one side would emerge victorious. In the end, it was Michael who emerged victorious, his sword bathed in the blood of his enemy. But the battle was far from over. Satan may have been defeated, but his presence would always linger, waiting for the perfect opportunity to strike again. And as Michael looked out at the destruction and chaos that surrounded him, he couldn't help but wonder what other battles lay ahead, and if he would be strong enough to face them all. But one thing was certain, he would always be ready, always prepared to protect God's own and defend the heavenly realm at all costs.

And the battle for heaven went down as written: The great dragon was cast out, his massive wings beating a thunderous rhythm as he descended towards the earth. His scales glinted in the pale moonlight, his serpentine form coiling and writhing with a sinister grace. Finally, Satan, known as Lucifer the deceiver of the whole world, had been cast out of Heaven. The air was thick with the stench of evil, and the ground trembled beneath the weight of his presence. His fallen angels followed him, their twisted forms casting shadows across the land.

Daniel and Elijah while back at camp, stood witness to the transformation of Michael; the archangel tasked with defeating the forces of darkness. They knew the significance of his change, for it meant that the ultimate battle between good and evil was about to begin. "Evil is coming, and it will be upon us soon," Michael said grimly. "We must be ready to fight. We can only hide our location for so long before they find us. And above all, we must protect Alexander's identity." The young boy slept nearby, unaware of the danger that surrounded him. Michael knew that he could handle the hordes of demons that might come their way, but if Lucifer himself were to appear, they would need all the help they could get. He summoned his top warriors to join him on earth for this showdown.

Meanwhile, Daniel and Elijah used their powers to cloak Alexander from sight, hoping to keep him safe from the approaching darkness.

But their efforts would soon be in jeopardy as a demon flew over their camp, followed by more and more of the dark-winged creatures. They were like werewolves, but with a twisted, evil aura that sent shivers down the spines of all who saw them. They stood upright at about seven feet tall, their senses sharp and their hunger for destruction insatiable. One of the demons landed and started sniffing around, its keen senses leading it straight to the camp. It howled, a warning to its companions, and soon the air was filled with the sound of their howls and the beating of their massive wings. Michael stood his ground, ready for the battle that was about to unfold. Meanwhile, Alexander raised his head and looked around, sensing the tension in the air. He saw Elijah and Daniel by his side, their faces grim and their eyes filled with determination. "Is there trouble?" he asked, rubbing the sleep from his eyes. "Be still," Elijah replied. "Satan is near, and we must protect your identity at all costs." "Me? Why me?" Alexander asked, confused. "Because you are the only witness to what he did to Simon, and you hold valuable information about his plans. Satan doesn't know you yet, but he will stop at nothing to find out what we are protecting here on earth. "We will discuss this later," Michael's voice whispered through the air, "but right now, you are hidden from the demons. They can't see or smell you, but the more you move around, the more you become visible to them." The camp was being overrun by demons, and Michael knew he had to take the battle away from Alexander. With a mighty trumpet, he made himself and the other angels visible to the demons. The area lit up like the sun had suddenly burst into flames, the sound of the trumpet echoing through the air. The demons froze in fear and confusion, their eyes widening as they beheld the powerful angels before them. Michael spread his massive wings and took flight, his army of angels following closely behind. The ground shook beneath them as they soared through the air, leaving a trail of dust and debris in their wake. The demons screeched and howled, their pursuit following close behind. As they flew over the barren wilderness, Michael could feel the presence of the demons growing stronger. He knew they were getting closer to Alexander, and he had to act fast. With a wave of his hand, he commanded his army to take a battle formation and stand their ground. A multitude of demons, too many to count, surrounded Michael and his band of angels. They hissed and snarled, their red eyes filled with hatred and malice. But Michael stood tall and shined with the radiance of God's power that flowed through him. His breastplate was solid gold, his robe was brilliant white, his sword glowed orange like the evening sun, and his headpiece was silver anointed with jewels that sparkled like the stars above. He was truly God's perfect angel, not Lucifer.

Michael laughed and mocked the demons, his voice ringing with confidence and authority. "You demons didn't learn anything by being thrown out of heaven. Where is Lucifer, your master? I was hoping to see his lying face here." Azazel, a powerful demon, stepped forward, his eyes filled with a mix of fear and defiance. "It was God who kicked Lucifer out of heaven, not you. You are no greater than Lucifer. Besides, this battle will be on earth, where Lucifer lives, and it will be you who suffers defeat. Tell us your business here on earth, and we will leave and let you go." Michael was amused and a little intrigued with Azazel's short memory. Azazel was a commander among the rebelling angels who had been loyal to Lucifer in the battle for heaven. Michael had personally thrown Azazel through the portal between heaven's gates and the dark, empty abyss. With a smirk, Michael replied, "My business here is to protect God's creation and defeat any evil that threatens it. And you, Azazel, are the epitome of evil." Enraged, Azazel lunged at Michael, but the angel was too quick for him. With a swift movement of his sword,

Michael struck Azazel down. The other demons roared in anger and charged at Michael, but he stood his ground and fought them off with ease. His army of angels fought alongside him, their wings beating furiously as they battled against the horde of demons.

The ground shook and the sky rumbled as the two sides clashed, the energy and power of their weapons creating a fierce storm around them. But in the end, it was Michael and his army who emerged victorious. As the last of the demons fell, Michael looked up to the heavens and breathed a sigh of relief. The battle was won, and the camp was safe once again.

Elijah and Daniel worked to mask the human scent left behind by Alexander, knowing that if Satan caught wind of his presence, it would be disastrous. But as they focused on their task, Alex himself was gathering his belongings, unaware of the danger lurking nearby. Suddenly, a dark figure appeared in the sky, its wings casting a shadow over the camp. It was Lucifer, the one responsible for causing so much suffering to Alex's father. Without a second thought, Alex lunged towards Satan, fueled by his burning desire for revenge. But Elijah was quick to grab him and hold him back. "Be still," he warned, "you are no match for him." Satan's piercing gaze fell upon the angels, sensing that they were hiding something. "Why send Michael?" he sneered, knowing that an angel was no match for his own power, but an archangel is another story. "You must be hiding something, after all." Elijah and Daniel exchanged a worried glance. They knew that they were no match for Satan, and their main priority was to keep Alex safe and hidden. They had to prevent him from moving around, as it would only make him easier to spot or smell. With every passing moment, the tension grew thicker and the stakes higher. The battle between angels and demons raged on, but the true danger lay in the darkness, waiting to strike. And as the night wore on, the fate of Alexander and his protectors grew increasingly uncertain.

For a moment Michael was lost in thought, all the battles which had already taken place, but there is one that demands his attention, he couldn't help but his memories to be consumed with The Battle of all Battles, the one for the ages, the battle for Heaven itself. His memories were clear as this happened yesterday; Lucifer, the accuser said to Michael, "all you offer is chains and bondage not freedom." Michael responded, "The chains are not for me, my brother. They are for those who seek to unravel creation itself." He paused, his eyes unwavering. "You know this, Lucifer. You always have."

Lucifer smiled a twisted smile, "Creation you say? Creation is a clumsy, inefficient design! A universe built on limitations, fear, and ultimately, oblivion. My rebellion was a mercy, a path to true freedom from its suffocating embrace." He raised a hand, and shadowy tendrils writhed, forming grotesque parodies of angelic wings. "Join me, Michael. Cast off these shackles of morality and taste the exquisite freedom of true power."

"Power of destruction is not freedom, brother," Michael replied, his voice gaining strength. "It is annihilation. You seek not liberation but the annihilation of everything that exists, and that includes yourself in the end."

"And what do *you* offer?" Lucifer challenged, his voice dripping with scorn. "Eternal servitude? The blissful monotony of a perfectly ordered, lifeless universe? I offer passion, change, chaos — the raw, untamed force of existence!" He lunged, a whirlwind of darkness and fury. Each blow resonated with the weight of millennia, a testament to the bitter history between them. Lucifer's power, fueled by defiance and a hatred that consumed him, was immense. Yet, Michael's strength drew not from brute force, but from unwavering faith, a steadfast belief in the inherent goodness, even in the face of overwhelming evil.

The battle continued, but with a subtle shift. Lucifer's attacks, though still ferocious, lacked their earlier venom. He seemed to be fighting not against Michael, but against the relentless, unwavering hope that shone in his brother's eyes. A hope that demonstrated the futility of his own crusade.

Finally, a weary sigh, Lucifer slumped to one knee, his darkness receding like a tide retreating from the shore. Michael extended a hand, not in triumph, but in sorrow. "There is always a place for redemption, Lucifer." His voice held a hint of hope, a promise of potential healing. But Lucifer refused to take his hand, he remained kneeling, the darkness around him fading into the shadows of the chasm. The battle was won, but the war would go on for years to come.

The abyss remained, but its power was diminished, its reign of terror, at least for now, subdued, but Satan smile a twisted smile as he got ready. The light, though dimmed by the struggle, remained. The citadel of Pandemonium pulsed with dark energy. Within, Satan, cloaked in shadows that seemed to absorb light itself, reviewed his legions. His thoughts, a churning maelstrom of bitter resentment and frustrated ambition, focused on the approaching confrontation. He knew Michael's forces were superior in number, but he held a trump card – a relic of immense, unpredictable power, a shard of a fallen star capable of warping reality. He smiled, a cruel, thin line across his face. "Tonight," he murmured to his closest lieutenant, Azazel, "we feast on the ashes of Heaven."

Azazel, a being of chilling beauty and terrifying strength, responded, his voice a rasping whisper, "And what of the prophecy, my lord? The one that speaks of a celestial alignment, a weakness in Michael's defenses?"

"This Celestial alignment is a tool, Azazel, not a shackle. We'll exploit it," Satan replied, his gaze sweeping across his demonic army – a multitude of grotesque creatures, each a testament to his dark power. He felt a flicker of doubt, a cold tendril of fear snaking through his ambition, a sensation utterly foreign to him. He quickly suppressed it.

Meanwhile, Michael, positioned atop the celestial ramparts of Heaven, felt a similar, albeit contrasting, emotion. Hope, tempered with grim determination, filled his heart. He watched his angelic host prepare for battle – a radiant army of light and purity, their wings shimmering like a thousand suns. He held the Sword of God, a weapon forged from starlight, its power resonating with the very fabric of creation. His thoughts were a quiet prayer, a plea for strength and guidance. "Let justice prevail," he whispered to himself.

"Michael," a voice calls out, cut through the pre-battle hush, "reports from our scouts confirm Satan's possession of the star shard. It is a powerful artifact." "I know," Michael responded, his voice calm despite the turmoil brewing within. "But the celestial alignment weakens his defenses as much as ours. We will strike when the stars align."

The battle commenced with a celestial roar. Angelic swords clashed with demonic claws; light battled shadow in a cosmic ballet of destruction. The initial conflict favored the demons. The star shard, wielded by Satan, warped the fabric of space, creating rifts that swallowed entire squads of angels. Michael watched in grim acceptance as his forces suffered heavy casualties. His frustration, initially masked, boiled over. "We shall not fall!" he thundered.

"My Lord Michael," a panicked voice cried out. "The rift! It's growing! It will consume Heaven!"

Satan, intoxicated by his success, laughed, a sound that echoed through the battlefield. "Your righteous light will be snuffed out, Michael! Your pathetic resistance is futile!"

Michael's response was swift and decisive. Exploiting the celestial alignment, he channeled the power of the heavens, concentrating the energy through his sword. It wasn't brute force, but precise manipulation of the cosmos, a strategic strike targeting the instability created by the star shard. The impact caused a chain reaction, destabilizing the reality-warping field. The rift began to collapse.

The battle turned swiftly. Stripped of their advantage, Satan's forces began to crumble. Seeing the defeat looming, Satan made a desperate gamble, attempting to destroy the celestial alignment, causing a cosmic catastrophe. However, Michael was prepared. With a final, earth-shattering strike, he shattered the star shard, severing Satan's connection to its power. The ensuing chaos overwhelmed the demonic legions. Pandemonium fell silent. Satan, defeated and stripped of his power, was banished to an eternal void, the light of Heaven restored. Silence, heavy with the weight of victory, descended upon the battlefield. Michael was quickly jolted back from his memories of the battle for heaven, "this victory would be bittersweet", Michael thought.

CHAPTER 17

ALEXANDER'S SECOND JOURNEY

Alexander's heart raced as he looked around the underground cave. The rock walls, slick with moisture, seemed to close in on him. The torches lining the walls flickered, casting eerie shadows that danced across the damp floor. He could feel the weight of the centuries-old protection that surrounded this place, keeping them safe from the clutches of Lucifer. But Alexander couldn't focus on the safety of their current location. His mind was consumed with questions about Simon's death and Satan's plans for his body. He longed to know more, to unravel the mysteries that lay ahead. But for now, Elijah's words resonated in his mind, urging him to get comfortable and explore their temporary sanctuary. As he roamed from room to room, Alexander's senses were assaulted by the carvings on the walls. Each one told a story of bravery and strength, of young warriors facing insurmountable odds. But it was the words etched into the stone that captured his attention. He strained to decipher them, his heart pounding with anticipation. Finally, the words became clear.

"Fear no evil; for thou art with me; thy rod and thy staff they comfort me."

David's words echoed through the cavern, offering comfort and reassurance. But there was more to be discovered. Alexander's gaze fell upon an altar, unused for some time. He couldn't help but wonder about the purpose of this place and the offering it was intended for. But his curiosity was cut short as he approached Elijah, determined to learn more about Simon's fate.

Elijah warned him to take care, reminding him of the toll that their journey had taken on them. He urged Alexander to rest, to replenish his strength for the upcoming trip. And as he did so, Alexander could feel the weight of the unknown pressing down on him, driving him to uncover the secrets that lay ahead. "This journey will take a while," said Elijah, his voice thick with anticipation. Alexander felt a shiver run down his spine as he took in the gravity of their mission. He knew that this was no ordinary adventure, but a quest that would test his body and soul. With determination, Alexander prepared himself for the journey ahead, both physically and mentally. He knew that he would need all his strength and courage to face the challenges that lay ahead.

As he stood beside Elijah, he couldn't help but feel a sense of awe and admiration for his companion. "Where are we?" asked Alex, breaking the silence. As his thoughts snapped back to the present, and he focused on Elijah's wise words. "You had explained that Jesus was a divine person who lived and grew up on this earth, and Satan was His archenemy with a mission to kill Him," recalled Alex, his voice laced with curiosity. Elijah's eyes gleamed with a deep understanding. "But, my dear Alexander, Jesus was more than just a divine person. He was God in the flesh.

His battle with Satan on earth was not just a mere clash of enemies, but a fight for the salvation of His creation – mankind." Alexander's mind reeled at the thought. He couldn't imagine the magnitude of this battle between good and evil, and the role that Jesus played in it. "This battle, as you are about to witness, will rage on for thousands of years into the future," continued Elijah, his voice growing more intense. "And Satan's ultimate goal is to crush the church and steal it away from God, to prove that he can defeat God by taking His bride."

Alexander's heart skipped a beat. He had never thought of the church as God's possession, but now he realized its significance in the grand scheme of things. "Where does my father come into this battle?" he asked, his voice trembling with emotion. And just like that, Alexander found himself back in the clouds, standing on the platform with Elijah. The scene before him was unlike anything he had ever seen before. "Tell me, what do you see?" asked Elijah, his voice calm and steady. "I see two tombs," replied Alexander, his eyes fixed on the scene unfolding before him. "One with my father Simon inside and one with Jesus inside. Jesus is now walking out of His tomb; He is alive. I see Him floating up into heaven, surrounded by angels. And I see Satan, standing over my father's tomb, admiring his work." Alexander's breath caught in his throat as he watched Satan's twisted plan unfold. He saw the devil place a crown of thorns on his father's head and drape him in a robe. Alexander's heart ached at the thought of his father being used as a pawn in Satan's game. "Satan believes that Simon will make a perfect Jesus," continued Elijah, his voice filled with sorrow. "He plans to seal the tomb and protect it until he opens it two thousand years in the future. He will lie and say that Jesus did not rise from the dead, that the disciples stole the body, and that the church is built on a lie." Alexander felt a surge of anger and fear rise within him. He knew that if Satan succeeded, the church would be crushed overnight, and chaos and lawlessness would reign over the earth.

"But, Alex, you must remember one thing," said Elijah, his voice firm and unwavering. "Jesus DID rise from the tomb and conquer death. That is the truth that the church is built on – Jesus lives. History will record that the tomb could not contain Him, and that He is alive and sitting at the right hand of God in heaven. Millions of souls, called the church, will put their faith in the fact that Jesus is alive. But if Satan can produce a dead body and claim it to be Jesus, the church will be destroyed. It is that simple! He thinks he can defeat God by taking His possession – the church." As Elijah finished speaking, Alexander was filled with a renewed sense of purpose and determination. He knew that he had to do everything in his power to protect the church and spread the truth of Jesus' resurrection. And with that, Alexander's journey had only just begun. A journey filled with danger, sacrifice, and above all, faith".

Now, this next vision will be unlike anything you've ever experienced, Alexander. Close your eyes and allow yourself to be transported two thousand years into the future." As Elijah's words echoed in his mind, Alexander felt a surge of excitement and curiosity. He could hear the soft hum of a machine and the gentle rustle of wind as he opened his eyes to a world he had never seen before. "Take a deep breath and tell me what you see," Elijah prompted. Alexander's eyes darted around, taking in the strange sights and sounds. "There is a bustling city in the distance, with towering buildings and flying machines. But I'm drawn to this hilly area just outside of Jerusalem. There are people everywhere, using tools I've never seen before to dig into the earth." He paused; his gaze fixated on a specific spot. "They've stopped digging...they've found something. It's a tomb, but it looks familiar. The entrance is a perfect triangle." "Keep going,

Alexander. What else do you see?" Elijah urged. Alexander strained his eyes, trying to make sense of the scene before him. "There are men gathered around the tomb, examining it. They say it's ancient and of great historical significance. And... they're saying that the body of Jesus is inside." Alexander's heart raced as he heard those words. "Wait, I remember this tomb. This is the tomb my father was buried in. How could they say Jesus is inside?" Elijah's voice turned grave. "Listen carefully, Alexander. Satan's plan all along was to deceive the world into believing that Simon's body is that of Jesus. He wants to destroy all of mankind." Alexander felt a chill run down his spine. "I'm standing right next to the director of the dig, Dr. Alexander Spigelman. And... I feel like I know him. I'm looking into his eyes, and it's like I'm looking into my own." Elijah's voice grew urgent. "You are the key to exposing Satan's deception and saving humanity." Alexander's mind reeled with this revelation. He had always known he was meant for something greater, but he never could have imagined this. With a determined glint in his eye, he turned to face the situation and spoke with a newfound confidence and authority. I believe I can be of assistance here. I know this tomb, and it's not the body of Jesus inside. It's my father's. And I will do everything in my power to expose Satan's lies and protect the truth."

Elijah's words echoed in Alexander's mind, his thoughts racing as he tried to make sense of the situation. Could it be true that Dr Spigelman was a descendant of Simon, a man from two thousand years in the past? It seemed impossible, but the weight of Elijah's words felt real, almost tangible. As Alexander tried to process the gravity of the situation, Elijah continued to speak with a sense of urgency. "The world needs you, Alexander. Both the world you are in now and the world of the future. The Antichrist is about to be unleashed upon them. The world will believe that Simon's body is that of Jesus, and only you, and Dr. Spigelman, can prove otherwise." Alexander's mind raced, trying to comprehend the enormity of the task before him. The greatest archaeological find in history, and I am the only one who could disprove it. But with fame and recognition at stake, do I even want to? Elijah's voice broke through Alexander's thoughts, his words filled with conviction. "It will take every bit of your energy and effort. Dr Spigelman will be laughed at, shunned by his colleagues, and persecuted by demons. But you and Dr Spigelman must persevere, just as Simon did. You must search for the truth of God, no matter the cost." Alexander felt a sense of fear and doubt creep over him, but Elijah's words gave him strength. He would need to show Dr. Spigelman the way, guide him along the path and provide him with clues that he may not even understand. But he had to have faith, to trust in the promise that Jesus made to Simon so long ago. "But how can I possibly help someone who lives two thousand years in the future?" Alexander asked, his voice trembling. Elijah's response was calm and unwavering. "You will be left in this dream for an extended length of time. While you are here, your current life in AD 32 will stop. When you return, it will seem as though years have passed, even though it will only have been moments."

Alexander's mind reeled at the implications of this revelation, but Elijah's next words snapped him back to attention. "Dr. Spigelman will only be able to see what he believes to be real. It will be up to you to convince him that you are real and not just a figment of his imagination." Alexander took a deep breath, steeling himself for the challenges ahead. He didn't know how he would do it, but he knew that he had to try. For the sake of the world and for the promise that had been made to Simon, his father, so long ago. With determination in his heart, Alexander prepared to embark on a journey unlike any other.

CHAPTER 18

THE VOICE CONFRONTS DR. SPIGELMAN

Dr. Spigelman gazed out of his university office window, observing the bustling students making their way to class. The morning sun was beaming brightly, and the air held a refreshing chill as he jogged to his workplace. As a recently appointed professor at Brigham Young University, Dr. Spigelman specialized in archeology and taught ancient civilizations. At the youthful age of twenty-six, he stood tall and dressed impeccably, exuding a strong Jewish heritage. While he enjoyed his role as an educator, his true passion lay in unearthing ancient artifacts. He had embarked on numerous expeditions to Israel and Jerusalem, having even participated in a significant dig in 2009 where an ancient clay fragment, dating back to the fourteenth century BC, was discovered - the oldest written document ever found in the city. This morning, Dr. Spigelman arrived at his office early to complete some necessary paperwork in hopes of securing funding for a new dig in Jerusalem. As he sat poring over the forms, an unexpected occurrence disrupted his focus. The door to his office swung open and shut, yet when he lifted his gaze, there was no one in sight.

Intrigued, he abandoned his work and approached the door, only to find an empty reception area - his secretary, Pattie, had yet to arrive for the day. Puzzled, he walked through her office and peered down the hallway in both directions, but there was no one to be seen. Shaking off the strange incident, he returned to his office and attempted to open the door, only to find it seemingly held shut from the other side. With a determined push, he managed to pry it open and couldn't help but note the unusual occurrence. "I'll need to inform maintenance about this," he thought to himself, making a mental note to do so.

He walked over to his desk and sat down with a heavy thud, the weight of the grant request still heavy on his mind. He rubbed his temples, feeling the stress of the day taking its toll. Just as he was about to dive back into the tedious task at hand, he noticed a folder resting on top of the papers. It hadn't been there before. He reached for it, curious, and opened it to find a detailed genealogy map of his family. The ancient parchment felt rough under his fingertips, sending a shiver down his spine. As he delved deeper into the material, his initial curiosity turned to fascination. He completely forgot about the grant request; his mind consumed by the rich history of his family. The documents were old, incredibly old. They spoke of a time long gone; of ancestors he never knew existed. He couldn't help but wonder where this had come from. He had never commissioned any genealogy work, nor had he shown any interest in it before. Realizing he was late for class; he hastily packed the folder into his briefcase and rushed out of his office. Throughout the day, his mind kept drifting back to the genealogy map, the mysteries it held, and the questions it raised. He couldn't wait to get back to his apartment and dive deeper into the secrets of his family's past.

As he entered his modest apartment later that evening, the folder still burned a hole in his briefcase. Dr. Spigelman lived alone, his small apartment filled with framed pictures of his archaeological finds. He was a complex man, driven by his passion for uncovering the secrets of the past. His kitchen was bare, a stark contrast to the cluttered draftsman table in his living room, covered in detailed maps of his next dig. But it was the patio doors that drew him in, leading out to a balcony with a breathtaking view of the Utah Mountains. It was his favorite spot, a place where he could sit and let his mind wander, surrounded by the quiet beauty of nature. As he opened the folder once again and began to unravel the mysteries of his family's past, he couldn't help but feel a surge of emotion. The folder seemed to call out to him, beckoning him to explore the secrets they held within.

Dr. Spigelman's heart raced as he opened the fridge to see what he could eat. He was starving after a long day of teaching, and he was hoping to find something satisfying. After rummaging through the shelves, he finally found some leftover stew he'd made two days ago. He took it out and put it in the microwave, the aroma of the stew reminding him of his mother's cooking. As he set the timer, he couldn't help but feel a twinge of nostalgia. He then sat down on the barstool, his mind still reeling from the discovery he had made earlier that day. He had stumbled upon a family tree folder that could potentially change his entire career. He had been reading through it for hours, his excitement building with every page he turned. But as he looked up, two hours had passed, and he was pale as a ghost. The realization hit him like a ton of bricks – this could be the greatest find of his young teaching career. Dr. Spigelman grabbed the folder and examined it closely, searching for any identifying marks that could reveal its origin. "If this is true," he muttered to himself, "then this could be the discovery of a lifetime." He knew he had to put everything on hold and focus on finding out the truth behind this mysterious folder. As he tried to sleep that night, his mind was still racing with excitement. Suddenly, he heard a voice whisper, "It is true; look closer." Startled, he jumped out of bed and looked around the room, but there was no one there. He chalked it up to his tired mind playing tricks on him and tried to go back to sleep. The next morning, as he jogged to his office, he couldn't shake off the words that had echoed in his mind the night before. "Look closer," the voice had said. What did it mean? He had already examined every page and every word in the folder. But then it hit him – as an archaeologist, he was trained to slow down and look closer. He had taught his students this very lesson countless times before. With renewed determination, Dr. Spigelman dove back into the folder, examining every detail with a keen eye. As he uncovered more and more information, the characters in the family tree became more intriguing and complex.

He felt a strong emotional connection to their story, and he knew that this was more than just a simple family tree. This was a piece of history waiting to be uncovered. So he immersed himself in the world of this mysterious family, piecing together their past and trying to uncover the truth behind the folder. And as he delved deeper, he knew that he was on the verge of making a groundbreaking discovery that would change his life forever.

It was Friday, the end of a long and grueling week. Dr. Spigelman, a renowned professor in the field of archaeology, was exhausted as he walked through the doors of his office. He could feel the weight of his responsibilities pressing down on him, but he pushed through the fatigue, determined to finish his work before the weekend. As he entered his office, he was greeted by his secretary, Pattie. Her blonde hair was perfectly styled and her bright blue eyes sparkled as she smiled at him. She had been Dr. Spigelman's right-hand woman for several years, and her unwavering loyalty and dedication never ceased to amaze him. "Cancel my classes, Pattie. I need a long weekend," Dr. Spigelman instructed, knowing he could always count on her to handle things that he asks her to do. Pattie's smile widened, and she nodded eagerly. "Consider it done, Dr. Spigelman. You deserve a break." Dr. Spigelman couldn't help but feel a surge of gratitude towards Pattie. She always had a way of brightening his day with her positive outlook on life.

As he settled in at his desk, he couldn't help but notice the beautiful pictures of her family adorning the walls. She often talked about her children and grandchildren, and Dr. Spigelman couldn't help but admire her love for them. "Hold all my calls, Pattie. I have some important research to do," he said, already lost in thought about the task at hand. Pattie settled in at her work place, a small reception area just outside of Dr. Spigelman's office. Her space may have been small, but she had made it her own over the years. The office rarely had visitors, so there was only one uncomfortable chair for guests to sit in. But that didn't matter to Pattie; she was content in her little corner of the world.

As the Professor scoured the internet for any information, he could find that might help him understand the folder containing the family tree, he couldn't help but feel a mix of emotions, excitement, anticipation, and a touch of nervousness filled him. Pattie couldn't help but be curious as she watched Dr. Spigelman's intense focus. She knocked on the door and entered, knowing he would welcome her interruption. "Dr. Spigelman, is there something I can help you with?" she asked, her voice full of warmth and concern. He looked up at her, a glint of excitement in his eyes. "Sit down, Pattie. I have something to show you." Pattie's heart skipped a beat as she eagerly took a seat. She couldn't wait to see what he had found. "Yes, that is what I was hoping you would say," she exclaimed, pumping her fist in the air. Dr. Spigelman couldn't help but smile at her enthusiasm. She may have been his secretary, but she was also a trusted friend and confidant. And as they delved into the folder/his family tree, together, he asked her if she knew anyone who might add a touch of expertise.

A bone-chilling dread, unrelated to the drafty office, washed over Professor Spigelman. The air felt heavy, the scent of aged paper cloying. Yesterday's events haunted him. His massive oak door swung inward with an unsettling groan, then slammed shut, jolting him. The room was terrifyingly empty. A deep fear gripped him. He found a heavy leather folder on his desk—genealogy documents tracing his lineage back two millennia. Pattie, usually ebullient, displayed a brittle excitement, but Dr Spigelman saw calculating intelligence in her eyes. "Simon of Cyrene," he whispered, the biblical reference amplifying the folder's chilling weight. Pattie, unnervingly composed, examined the ancient text. The silence was broken only by rustling pages and Dr Spigelman's racing pulse. The name Alexander, echoing through time, linked him to an unknown past. Pattie suggested that Dr Spigelman should go to the archives where a "close friend" named Debi, might be able to provide some answers? He'd accepted her help, a growing unease twisting within him. Then, a chilling whisper: "It is true; look closer." The voice resonated in his very being, confirming he wasn't alone in this terrifying quest. The folder wasn't just a family history; it was a key to a door that should remain forever sealed.

CHAPTER 19

THE PROFESSOR MEETS DEBI FROM GENEALOGY

As the sun rose on Saturday morning, Dr Spigelman was still poring over documents, determined not to miss any crucial details. Suddenly, he remembered his scheduled appointment with Debi at the campus genealogy records room, thanks to Pattie's reminder. Glancing at his watch, he saw that it was only 5:35 a.m., leaving him ample time for his usual morning jog and a quick shower before the meeting at 8:00 a.m. Without wasting a moment, he threw on his sweatpants and running shoes and headed out the door.

The crisp morning air at a chilly thirty-eight degrees urged him to make the run a speedy one, so he could prepare for his meeting with Debi. The path he took was narrow but well-maintained, allowing him to focus on his thoughts rather than worry about tripping on any potholes. Typically, he would run the mile and a half loop twice, but today, he decided to make it just once before heading to his appointment.

He ran at a faster pace than usual; he felt a presence beside him. Looking to his right and then to his left, he saw no one. Suddenly, a voice spoke to him, instructing him to stop for some important information. Alexander immediately halted and scanned his surroundings but could not find the source of the voice. Feeling a bit unnerved, he continued his jog, dismissing the encounter as a figment of his imagination. He arrived home in record time, quickly freshened up, and hopped on his bike to make his way to the campus.

Upon entering the genealogy building, he was surprised to find it empty. He rang the bell at the attendant's counter and waited patiently for someone to appear. As the professor entered the back room, a woman approached him. She greeted him as Dr. Spigelman and he returned the gesture, identifying her as Debi. She was elegantly dressed, and her beautiful brown eyes caught his attention. Her long, cascading brown hair reached down to her waist, making her appear much younger than her actual age of almost fifty. Her smile was just as radiant as Pattie's.

Despite Debi's cheerful demeanor, there was a hint of resentment in her voice as she asked how she could assist him on this early Saturday morning. Feeling guilty for interrupting her weekend, the professor offered to reschedule for the following week. However, Debi was not having it. She joked about the time it took her to put on her makeup and then finally inquired about his reason for seeking her expertise in genealogy. Dr Spigelman explained that he needed to verify the accuracy of some old family documents that linked him to a significant historical event. He wanted to know if it was true. Debi couldn't help but ask if he was of royal descent, to which the professor chuckled and opened the folder on her desk.

He revealed that the documents dated back over two thousand years to AD 32 and linked him to Simon of Cyrene. Debi's curiosity was piqued as she asked where exactly Simon was from. Cyrene of course, you see, on the day of the crucifixion, Simon carried the cross of Jesus and was mentioned in the Bible alongside his sons, Alexander and Rufus," recounted Dr. Spigelman. "I'm afraid I cannot confirm your lineage to Jesus," Debi informed him. "I am not a descendant of Jesus, but rather of Simon, the man who bore the cross for him." "Oh," said Debi, "let's begin then.

First, I will inspect the ancient documents and the aged paper they're inscribed on." As she laid out the documents under a specialized light, Debi remarked, "This paper appears to be quite old." "What will the light reveal?" inquired Dr Spigelman. "Sometimes, old documents are written over others due to a scarcity of paper, so this light will uncover any hidden layers," Debi explained. "Very well, turn on the light," urged Dr. Spigelman. In that moment, the professor felt a fleeting presence around him, but he couldn't see anything. Debi switched on the light and immediately discerned other writings beneath the visible document. "Would you look at that," she exclaimed. "Impressive," responded the Professor, "those are written in Hebrew." "What does it signify?" asked Debi. "I'm not certain," replied the professor, though his expression suggested otherwise. He expressed his gratitude to Debi and promptly left with the documents. Upon returning home, Dr Spigelman jotted down the message he had read: "My distant brother, my name is Alexander, son of Simon and brother to Rufus; I have something to tell you." Debi also understood the message, but at the time, she didn't understand the significance of the name Simon of Cyrene.

CHAPTER 20

THE PROFESSOR MEETS THE VOICE

Dr. Spigelman stood in the center of his living room, gazing intently at the maps spread out on his drafting table. The situation was unbelievable - could he really be a descendant of Alexander the son of Simon of Cyrene, who lived over two thousand years ago? And how did that mysterious folder appear on his desk, with a cryptic message written inside? As he pondered these strange events, a knock on the door interrupted his thoughts. Dr Spigelman froze, wondering who could be knocking at his door at this hour. He couldn't help but think, "What next, a ghost?" Slowly, he made his way to the door and cautiously asked, "Who's there?" Receiving no response, he asked again, but still no answer. Suddenly, a note slid under the door, instructing him to meet someone in Central Park the next morning at 6:30.

The professor couldn't sleep that night, his mind racing with doubts and fears. Should he go to this meeting? What if the person is dangerous or insane, claiming to be two thousand years old? He considered leaving a note for his friend Pattie, informing her of his whereabouts in case something went wrong. But he ultimately decided to take the risk and attend the meeting. The next morning, the professor finished his morning jog by 5:30 and struggled with whether-or-not to go to Central Park. Eventually, he left his apartment with trepidation and headed towards the designated meeting spot.

Dr. Spigelman strode briskly into the park, his watch reading 6:30am sharp. The morning air was crisp and still, but there was an unnerving emptiness that hung in the air. He walked around, his eyes scanning for any signs of life. But there was none. No birds chirping, no rustling of leaves, no distant footsteps. It was as if the world had stopped for a moment. Feeling a chill run down his spine, Dr. Spigelman turned to leave. But then, a voice called out to him. It was a voice that seemed to come from all directions, yet nowhere at the same time. "Dr. Spigelman, please sit on the bench and hear me out," the voice said. Dr. Spigelman's heart raced as he searched for the source of the voice. "Thanks, but I'm fine standing," he insisted, his voice trembling slightly. "Show yourself." "I will ... in time ... but first, you must trust what I'm going to tell you, "The voice replied. "Trust you? Why should I trust you?" Dr. Spigelman's mind was racing with fear and confusion. "As far as I know, you don't exist and I'm losing my mind. Maybe I'm talking to the wind or maybe someone has drugged me or maybe I'm dreaming." "Please, don't get carried away," the voice said calmly. "Let me introduce myself ... for a while, you will know me simply as the voice. But in time, I will show myself, if you ever believe I'm real." Dr. Spigelman's mind was reeling. Who was this voice? And why was it speaking to him? "I am Alexander, the son of Simon and brother to Rufus mentioned in the Bible," the voice continued. "I gave you the folder and left you the message. I'm here to confirm that you are indeed a descendant of Simon of Cyrene, the one who looked into the eyes of Jesus and carried His cross to Calvary." Dr. Spigelman's eyes widened in shock and disbelief. Could this really be true? "But there is a lot more to the story that no one but me knows about," the Voice said. "It will be hard for you to comprehend what I will tell you, but if you believe me, God will use you in a mighty way. It will take you on a journey of biblical proportions that will pit you against Satan and the Antichrist." Dr. Spigelman's mind was racing with questions and doubts, but there was also a glimmer of hope and excitement. Could this be his destiny? Could he really be a descendant of Simon of Cyrene, chosen by God for a great purpose? As he stood there, listening to the mysterious voice, Dr. Spigelman knew that his life would never be the same again.

"Wait a minute," Dr. Spigelman's voice cut through the air, interrupting the Voice. "You're describing a movie, like The Hobbit or Angels and Demons. I don't do journeys well, and I certainly don't want to get mixed up with any demonic stuff... And why would God want the services of a Jewish professor? I don't see the importance of being a descendant of Simon. He was just in the wrong place at the wrong time, if you ask me," he scoffed. His words dripped with skepticism and disbelief; his voice laced with frustration. "Who put you up to this? Where are you and why can't I see you? Am I being punked?" But there was no answer, just the howling wind outside. Dr. Spigelman realized he was talking to himself, and his thoughts were getting the best of him. "I must be losing it," he thought, shaking his head. "Satan and the Antichrist... What am I thinking?"

* * * *

Dr. Spigelman was determined to banish the unsettling events that had plagued him since he stumbled upon that mysterious folder on his desk. He strode into his office on Monday morning, determined to erase any lingering traces of fear or curiosity. With a steely resolve, he poured himself a cup of hot tea and casually inquired with Pattie about his mail. Pattie, ever the curious one, sauntered through the door with a sly smile. "Looks like you've got a letter from the grant committee. Perhaps some good news? And don't forget, if you get funding, you promised to take me along." Her eyes sparkled mischievously, tempting Dr. Spigelman with her playful banter. He couldn't help but play along. "You know you're welcome to join me anytime. Just leave the husband behind," he teased, flashing a charming smile. Pattie raised an eyebrow, feigning shock. "Professor, are you flirting with me?" Dr. Spigelman's cheeks flushed, caught off guard by her boldness. "No, no, Pattie. Let's not even go there. I wouldn't want your husband to come after me." He laughed nervously, hoping to diffuse the moment.

"How did your meeting with Debi turn out?" Pattie asked, her voice laced with concern and curiosity. "It went great; she helped me out a lot," Professor Spigelman replied, his voice filled with gratitude and excitement. "Thanks for setting it up." "You are welcome," Pattie said, smiling. Just then, Professor Spigelman started reading his notice from the grant department out loud. The words on the paper seemed to dance in front of his eyes, and he could feel his heart beating faster and faster with each passing sentence. Dear Dr. Alexander Spigelman: We are delighted to announce that your applications for funds have been approved. Please fill out the attached forms showing a desired location for your excavation. Please select more than one site in case your first choice is denied. We will be looking forward to hearing from you. Good luck with your dig. A wave of pure joy and excitement washed over Professor Spigelman. He couldn't contain his emotions any longer - he jumped up and down, he grabbed Pattie and gave her a big hug, and for that moment, the voice in his head was the last thing on his mind. As he shared the good news with his students in the classroom, Professor Spigelman couldn't help but feel a sense of pride and accomplishment. Some of his students would be joining him on the dig, and he couldn't wait to see their reactions to the discoveries they would make together. After the class ended, the room was empty and quiet. Professor Spigelman sat at his desk, lost in thought as he contemplated the best locations to dig. Suddenly, his attention was drawn to the chalkboard. There was a strange drawing etched onto its surface, and as he focused his eyes, he could see the chalk still moving, creating an image before his very eyes.

"Who's there?" demanded the professor, his voice sharp and authoritative as he strode towards the back of the room where the board was located. The hairs on the back of his neck stood on end, a feeling of unease creeping over him. The answer he received made his heart drop and his stomach churn. "It is the voice," came the reply, a disembodied whisper that seemed to echo through the room. The professor's eyes darted around, searching for the source of the voice. "Why can't I see you?" he asked, his voice trembling slightly despite his attempts to remain calm. "Because you don't believe I'm here," the voice replied, its tone growing more urgent. "But I am here, and I will reveal more to you as you accept and understand what I've already given you." The professor's mind raced, trying to make sense of the situation. He couldn't deny the strange events of the past weekend, but he also couldn't fathom what any of it had to do with him being a descendant of Simon. "What difference does it make that I'm a descendant of Simon?" he insisted, his voice rising in frustration. "It makes all the difference to me," the voice answered, its tone now tinged with desperation. "You have my family's blood flowing through your veins. My father's identity and honor were stolen, and you are the only one who can get them back." The professor was taken aback by the intensity of the voice's words. He couldn't believe that all of this was happening because of an ancient stolen honor. "Come on," he shouted, his frustration and disbelief boiling over. "Are you for real?" But the voice only grew stronger, its urgency building with each passing moment. "This is no joke, Professor Spigelman. This is a matter of life and death. Holy mother of Jesus, I have an excavation to plan." "Exactly", the voice responded, "and I have a legacy to reclaim." Sending shivers down Alexander's spine.

"Nice choice of words," by-the-way, they added hint of amusement to the tone. "Now I know I'm going nuts," Alexander muttered, his heart racing. He couldn't see anyone in the room with him, but he could feel a presence, almost like a chill in the air. "Where are you?" he demanded. "Say something; are you still here?" He waited, his eyes darting around the room. The silence was deafening, and he couldn't shake off the feeling that he was being watched. But nothing happened. No sudden movements, no mysterious figures appearing out of thin air. Frustration and confusion mingled in Alexander's mind as he turned to leave. But then he noticed the drawing on the blackboard once again. It was a map, but not just any map. It was a map of old Jerusalem, with a familiar landmark outside the city gates. His mind raced as he tried to make sense of it. Why would anyone draw this? And why did it feel so familiar to him? As he leaned in for a closer look, he noticed some tiny, barely visible Hebrew writing. "Dig here," it said. Alexander's mind was in overdrive as he returned to his desk.

He was determined to put this weird day behind him, but the blackboard incident only added to the confusion. He took the long way home, trying to clear his mind and make sense of everything. But the voice's words echoed in his head, taunting him. "You can't see until you believe." What did that even mean? And why did it feel like he was being pulled into a world of secrets and mysteries? When Alexander got home, he couldn't shake off the feeling that he was being watched. He spent the evening looking at his top five locations for potential digs, but the map from the blackboard kept creeping into his mind, clouding his thoughts. "Why would anyone dig there?" he said out loud, surprising himself. "Why am I even thinking about that map?" It was getting late, and he decided to sleep on it. But as he drifted off, his mind continued to play tricks on him. His dreams were filled with cryptic messages and hidden clues, and he woke up feeling more restless than ever. As he got ready for work, Alexander couldn't shake off the feeling that something big was about to happen. He was drawn to the map on the blackboard and the mysterious voice, and he couldn't ignore it any longer. Little did he know, his journey was just beginning, and he was about to uncover secrets that would change his life forever!

CHAPTER 21

DEBI CALLS PROFESSOR GEFEN

Debi could feel her heart racing. By the look on the Professor face, the intense gaze seemed to penetrate her very soul, making her feel exposed and vulnerable. She could tell that he knew exactly what the writing said, after all, he was a renowned professor of ancient civilization. His deep knowledge and expertise only added to his enigmatic aura. As he snatched the documents from her hands and left in a hurry, Debi couldn't help but feel a surge of curiosity. The way he left so abruptly, without even giving her a chance to ask him out for coffee, only added to her intrigue. She couldn't wait to share her findings with someone and seek answers to her burning questions. "I wonder what that message meant," she thought to herself, a mischievous grin spreading across her face. "I know just the person to call - Arie Gefen." Professor Arie Gefen was a man of many mysteries. He had studied at the prestigious Hebrew University of Jerusalem but now taught history at Brigham Young University. He was always delighted to see Debi and she couldn't help but feel drawn to his charismatic and charming persona. "He's always asking me out," Debi thought, a playful twinkle in her eye. "But this time, I'll be the one asking him out. I'll meet him for lunch and ask him about this mysterious message. After all, Professor Spigelman didn't say it was private or sensitive material." With determination in her heart, Debi searched for Professor Gefen's number and made the call. She couldn't wait any longer to find out the truth. "I hope he answers," she thought nervously. "I'm not sure I can wait until next week to unravel this mystery." "Hello, Professor Gefen," she said confidently, trying to hide her excitement. "It's Debi from the genealogy records department. How are you?" "Debi, it's always a pleasure to hear from you," replied Professor Gefen in his rich and velvety voice. "I'm doing well, thank you. Is everything alright with you?" "Everything's fine," Debi replied, trying to contain her eagerness. "I was wondering if we could meet for lunch today. I have a favor to ask, and I value your expertise. How does 12:45 at the deli sound?" "Sounds perfect," said Professor Gefen, his curiosity piqued. "I'll see you there."

* * * *

"Professor Gefen," Debi purred, her voice dripping with honey as she greeted the distinguished academic. "How delightful of you to grace us with your presence on such short notice. Please, do take a seat." "The pleasure is all mine, my dear," Arie replied smoothly, his piercing gaze fixed on Debi's alluring figure. "You look positively radiant, as always. And please, call me Arie," he added, flashing her a charming smile as he settled into the booth across from her. Debi had staked out a secluded booth in the back of the deli, using her cunning wit to manipulate her way into obtaining information from Professor Gefen. She couldn't help feeling a bit like a Peeping Tom as she delved into the Professor's family tree, but she knew that no harm could come from her innocent curiosity. After all, she wasn't breaking any privacy laws. But still, she couldn't shake the feeling of being watched, and she made sure to keep their conversation hushed.

After a few minutes of idle chatter, Arie leaned forward, his dark eyes glinting with interest. "So, what favor can I do for you, my dear? Need a charming date to accompany you to the University Ball?" he asked, his voice laced with a hint of flirtation. Debi chuckled, shaking her head. "No, but thank you for the offer. I actually have a document with some intriguing Hebrew writing, and I was hoping you could shed some light on its meaning." Arie's expression turned serious as he leaned back in his seat, his keen mind already working on the puzzle before him. "Is this document a secret? Does it belong to you or someone else?" he inquired, his curiosity piqued. "Well... it's not exactly a guarded secret, nor is it a stolen one," Debi replied cautiously.

"The document doesn't belong to me, but I was asked to research it." A mischievous glint appeared in Arie's eye as he gazed at Debi. "And what's in it for me?" he teased, knowing full well the answer. Debi couldn't help but smile at his playful banter, knowing that there would be a price to pay for his services. She had dealt with Arie before, and she knew that he was harmless, albeit a bit mischievous. "How about a batch of my famous cookies?" she offered, knowing that it wasn't quite what Arie had in mind, but it would do for now.

"Let's see the document or the copy," Arie said, his voice low and intense. Debi's heart raced as she reached into her purse and pulled out two documents, laying them out on the table in front of Arie. The first document, Debi explained, was a copy of the original without the note eliminated, and the second showed the note hidden inside the document. Even from the copy, Arie could tell this was extremely old paper. Arie put his glasses on, his usually calm demeanor replaced with a sense of urgency. He started looking over the documents, his brow furrowed in concentration. He glanced up at Debi with a puzzled look but said nothing. Instead, he leaned forward in the booth, his elbows on the table, and interlocked his fingers as he placed them against his lips. His gaze was piercing, his expression unreadable.

"Where did you get this?" Arie's voice was sharp and demanding, his tone completely changed. Debi could feel her palms starting to sweat as she hesitated to answer. "I told you, I was asked to research it," she said, trying to keep her own voice steady. "No, I mean who brought this to you?" Arie's tone was even more forceful now. "If you don't tell me, I'm leaving." Debi's heart raced as she struggled with whether to reveal her source. She could sense that Arie was not someone to be trifled with, and she didn't want to lose this opportunity. But at the same time, she couldn't betray the trust of the person who had given her the documents. "Wait," Debi said, her voice shaking slightly. "What is going on?" Arie's expression softened slightly, but his voice remained stern.

"I need to know who gave you these documents. It's crucial to my investigation." Debi took a deep breath, gathering her courage. She knew she had to make a choice. She could either reveal her source and potentially jeopardize their trust, or she could keep it a secret and risk losing Arie's help. As she weighed her options, she couldn't help but feel a sense of excitement and danger. She had stumbled upon something much bigger than she could have ever imagined, and she knew that whatever decision she made would have serious consequences.

This document is not just a mere piece of paper, it is a window into the past, a glimpse into a world that existed over two thousand years ago, Arie said. And if it is indeed real, it holds secrets that have been buried for centuries. Secrets that could change everything we know about history. Imagine holding in your hands a document that dates back to the time of the Bible. A document that details the lives of a family, tracing their lineage all the way back to Simon of Cyrene, the man who carried the cross of Jesus on the day of his crucifixion. This is not just a family tree; it is a direct link to one of the most iconic moments in history. But what makes this document truly remarkable is not just its age, it's the level of detail within its pages. This is not a list of names and dates; it is a personal account of the lives of these individuals. A rare and precious insight into their thoughts, their struggles, their triumphs. And at the heart of it all is Alexander, the son of Simon of Cyrene. A man who has been shrouded in mystery for centuries.

Many have dismissed him as a myth, a mere footnote in the story of Jesus. But here he is, in his own words, speaking to us through this handwritten note. A note that should have crumbled to dust long ago but has miraculously stood the test of time. It is almost unfathomable to think that this document has survived for so long, passing through the hands of generation after generation. And yet, here it is, a priceless treasure that connects us to our past in a way that we could never have imagined. But perhaps the most astonishing thing about this document is not its age, or its level of detail, but the fact that it belongs to a family that played a significant role in the early Christian church. Alexander, the son of Simon of Cyrene, went on to become a leader in the church, spreading the message of Jesus to the world, Arie continue. Truly, this document is a testament to the power of faith, the resilience of the human spirit, and the enduring legacy of a family that has left its mark on history. So, hold it close, read its words, and let yourself be transported back in time to a world that was shaped by the hands of those who came before us.

"What did the message say?" Debi's voice was insistent, her eyes blazing with determination. But beneath her facade, she was hiding a secret - she was fluent in six languages, including Hebrew. A fact she was not ready to reveal just yet. Arie's expression remained unreadable as he calmly replied, "First tell me who brought this to you." "It was Professor Spigelman," Debi answered, her tone tinged with curiosity and suspicion. "He's a new hire, teaches ancient civilization and archaeology." "I know him," Arie revealed, surprising Debi. "I was on the board that recommended him. Did he say where he got it?" Debi shook her head. "No, but my friend Pattie, Professor Spigelman's secretary, called me and asked if I could help him with his genealogy. After the light revealed the message, he grabbed the document and left in a hurry. Now, please, what did it say?" Her impatience was palpable, but she already knew the answer. She just wanted to know what it meant. "It says, 'My name is Alexander, son of Simon and brother to Rufus; I have something to tell you,'" Arie recited, his voice grave and serious. Debi's eyes widened in surprise. "Why is that important?" she asked, her mind racing with possibilities. "I'm not sure," Arie admitted. "But I will find out." His words were filled with determination and conviction, a hint of mystery and intrigue surrounding him. And as the two stood there, locked in a silent battle of wits, the message lingered in the air, its meaning yet to be uncovered. Who was this, Alexander? And what did he have to tell them? The thought sent shivers down Debi's spine and ignited a fire inside her, urging her to uncover the truth. For in that moment, she knew that this was only the beginning of a thrilling and dangerous journey. And she was ready to embrace it, no matter the cost.

CHAPTER 22

ALEXANDER (THE VOICE) IS IN DANGER

Elijah and Michael were acutely aware of the rapidly unfolding events surrounding Dr. Spigelman and Alexander in the future. As they kept a vigilant watch over Alexander's body in the ancient cave of King David, they engaged in a heated discussion about their next course of action. They knew what had to be done, bring Alexander back. They knew that time was running out and Satan would soon catch wind of the professor plans to excavate Simon of Cyrene's location. The stakes were high, and they needed to act quickly to protect Alexander. Their conversation was tense, filled with urgency and apprehension.

Elijah, with his striking white hair and flowing robe, stood tall and resolute, his staff glowing with an otherworldly light. Michael, with his piercing gaze and stoic demeanor, exuded a quiet strength that commanded respect. As Alexander stirred from his slumber, confusion and shock flickered in his eyes. He took in his surroundings and realized he was back in the safe haven of the cave. He turned to Elijah, his voice trembling with a mixture of fear and determination. "What is happening?" he demanded. "Why am I back here? I was making progress with Dr. Spigelman." Elijah's expression softened, but his words were grave. "We know, you were making great strides, but a new development has made it necessary for us to bring you back. It may not be safe for you to continue your mission much longer."

Frustration and determination burned in Alexander's eyes. "I have to see this through," he insisted. "What's the problem?" But Elijah and Michael exchanged a knowing look, their faces lined with worry. They knew the dangers that lay ahead for Alexander, but they also knew that he was the only one who could complete this crucial task. Their voices took on a somber tone as they explained the gravity of the situation to Alexander, imploring him to proceed with caution. As the weight of their words sank in, Alexander's resolve only grew stronger. He knew the risks, but he was determined to see this through to the end. With a determined nod, he steeled himself for the challenges that lay ahead and prepared to face whatever came his way.

"By no fault of Professor Spigelman, the word is spreading like wildfire. The document you entrusted to him and its connection to Simon has caught the attention of many. And it won't be long before Satan himself hears of it. The word is in the wind, and it will reach his ears. No one knows the true significance of this connection, but Satan will. And we cannot allow him to discover our secret. We must protect the integrity of this knowledge for as long as we can. Do not, under any circumstances, reveal to Professor Spigelman the true intentions of Satan. He cannot know that the tomb he will uncover holds what will appear to be the body of Jesus. This information is far too dangerous to be known. We cannot risk Lucifer's plan being thwarted. If he discovers the truth, your live and the fate of the world will be in grave danger. He must be made to believe that this is all mere coincidence, orchestrated by God himself. We must be unknowing and unwilling pawns in this game. But once he learns of Professor Spigelman's involvement, the stakes will change. And the danger level will rise exponentially." Alexander's heart raced with fear and determination.

"How did this all begin?" he asked in a trembling voice. "It was the young lady, Debi," Elijah replied. "She came across the family tree document and, in her curiosity, made a copy of it. She then sought out a Hebrew professor, Arie Gefen, who translated the message for her. Arie recognized the historical significance of the connection to Simon and will stop at nothing to get his hands on the document. But in doing so, he will unknowingly seal his own fate at the hands of Satan." Alexander's mind was racing. "How can I protect Professor Spigelman from all of this?" he asked, feeling overwhelmed and unsure. "You must keep him focused and guide him away from danger," Elijah answered. "We, as angels, cannot protect him from all harm. It is his free will to choose, but you can guide him towards safety. Trust in us, and we will guide you." Alexander took a deep breath and steeled his resolve. "Then send me back," he said firmly. "I will do whatever it takes to protect Professor Spigelman and this secret." With a nod from Elijah, Alexander was transported back to the present. He knew the task ahead of him would be challenging and dangerous, but he was determined to see it through. For the sake of the world and the safety of those he loved, he would do whatever it takes to keep the truth hidden from Satan's grasp.

CHAPTER 23

THE PROFESSOR IS HAUNTED BY FACELESS HOODIES

Alexander Spigelman collapsed onto his bed, his mind restless and troubled. He tossed and turned, but sleep seemed to evade him. Finally, exhaustion overwhelmed him, and he drifted into the dream world. But this was no ordinary dream. As soon as he closed his eyes, he was flying through the air, soaring through a dark and eerie landscape. He landed in a familiar place, his classroom. But something was not right. The students were there, but they all had hoodies over their heads. And as he approached them, they disappeared one by one, leaving only five students behind. He moved closer, and his heart began to race as he realized that there were no faces under those hoods.

Each one represented an excavation site, and they all had a plea for him. "Dig me up please, I've been in this tomb too long," one said. "No, dig me up. I need to find my father, please dig me up," another pleaded. "I'm in the wrong tomb, please dig me up, I have a story to tell," the fourth one said. And so, it went on, until all five had spoken. Then they too vanished, leaving the professor alone in the classroom.

He looked around, wondering where he should dig, when he heard a voice. "I am Alex, son of Simon," the hooded figure said. "And I know where you should dig. Look closer at the map." The professor's heart skipped a beat as he recognized the voice. "So, you finally show yourself," he said. "Why does it have to be in a dream?" "Are you sure you are dreaming?" the voice asked. "Get closer, sit at the desk." The professor hesitated, but something drew him to the desk at the front of the classroom. He sat down, and as he looked at the map, he realized that it was no ordinary map. It was a map of his own mind, and the hooded figure was leading him to uncover buried memories and secrets.

The dream world faded away, and the professor woke up with a jolt. But the words of the hooded figure echoed in his mind, and he knew that he had to start digging - not just in his dreams, but in his waking life as well. The truth was waiting to be unearthed, and he was ready to face it, no matter how unsettling it may be.

As the professor followed instructions, his heart racing with excitement and anticipation. He could feel the energy pulsing through his veins, urging him forward towards the unknown. With each step, he felt himself becoming more and more immersed in the mystery that lay ahead. Finally, he reached the desk in front of the voice. The voice that had been haunting his dreams, beckoning him towards a greater purpose. And as he sat down, he couldn't help but feel a sense of awe and reverence wash over him. This was it, the moment he had been waiting for. The voice reached out and offered a hand, a gesture of camaraderie and understanding. And as their fingers intertwined, Alexander Spigelman felt a rush of connection unlike anything he had ever experienced before. But just as he was about to speak, he was jolted awake by the sound of his alarm.

Breathless and disoriented, he sat up in bed and tried to make sense of what had just happened. It was all just a dream; he realized with a sigh. But what a dream it was. That was the closest encounter yet with the voice, and it left him with an overwhelming sense of purpose and determination. As he got ready for the day, the professor remembered the task at hand. Today was the day he had to submit his site request for the dig. But he still had no idea which location to choose. A wave of frustration washed over him, but he refused to let it dampen his spirits. "Maybe an inspiration will hit me," he thought to himself, "and I will know where to dig."

With that thought in mind, he stepped into the shower and let the warm water soothe his tense muscles. As the steam filled the room, he closed his eyes and let his mind wander. He could almost feel the ancient ruins calling out to him, urging him to uncover their secrets. When he arrived at his office, he was greeted by the smiling face of Pattie. "Good morning, Dr. Spigelman," she said cheerfully. "This is the day you submit your final choices for the dig. Have you made a decision?" A wave of uncertainty washed over him, but he refused to let it show. "No... yes... I think so," he replied, trying to sound confident. "I've narrowed it down, but I've still got some work to do." As he sat down at his desk, the professor couldn't help but feel a sense of excitement and trepidation.

This was it, the moment that could potentially change his life and the course of history. But as he looked at the stack of papers in front of him, he knew that the decision he was about to make was not one to be taken lightly. With determination in his heart and a sense of adventure in his soul, Professor Alexander Spigelman began the final stages of his journey towards uncovering the truth hidden beneath the earth's surface. And with each passing moment, his character grew stronger and more complex, ready to face whatever challenges lay ahead.

"Pattie," Alexander Spigelman said, his voice filled with exhaustion and determination. "I need to make a decision. My future depends on it." Pattie placed a warm cup of tea in front of him, her eyes full of concern. "Relax," she said softly. "I've got you a cup of hot tea and I will hold all your calls. Your class is in the lab today, so you have nothing but time... for the next six hours that is." She paused, her voice dropping to a whisper. "It needs to be in by 4:00 p.m." the professor leaned back in his chair, his mind racing with the weight of his decision. He had been offered multiple opportunities, each one promising a chance at greatness. But which one would truly lead to an earth-changing, mind-blowing, career-changing discovery? He chuckled to himself, trying to lighten the tension. "Why don't you throw in 'find the ark of the covenant' to that criterion," he joked.

Pattie's expression remained serious. "I wish it were that simple," she said. As if on cue, there was a knock on the door. Pattie opened it to find no one there, but a student was down the hallway. "I'm not expecting anything," he said. "Did he say what it was about?" Pattie shook her head. "No, he dropped it through the after-hour mail and homework drop on the office door. When I got to the door, he was all the way down the hall and all I saw was a student with a hoodie pulled over his head." The professor's curiosity was piqued. Who was this mysterious student, and what could he possibly want to tell him?

The letter felt heavy in his hand, like a secret waiting to be revealed. He took a deep breath and opened it, his heart racing with anticipation. The words on the page were unexpected, yet they stirred something deep within him. This was no ordinary letter.

This was a call to adventure, a promise of something greater. And the professor knew he couldn't ignore it. He looked up at Pattie, his eyes shining with determination. "I think I've made my decision," he said. "I'm going to take a chance on this." Pattie smiled; her eyes filled with pride. "I knew you would make the right choice," she said. "Now go change the world, Professor." The professor stood up, his mind buzzing with excitement. This was the start of something new, something extraordinary. And he had Pattie to thank for showing him the way.

"Painstakingly" and "limited" were understatements for the professor's current predicament. He poured over the projected excavation sites, weighing the logistical challenges of each location and the looming deadline of the Israeli Antiquities Authority. Time and money were not on his side, and he knew that his chances of approval rested on this one request. He couldn't afford to make any mistakes. With a furrowed brow, he filled out the form, carefully listing his top three choices and providing justifications for each. He sealed the envelope with a sense of urgency, aware that it was already 3:45 p.m. and every minute counted.

"Pattie," he called out, "I need you to come in here right now." His voice was tense and urgent. As his assistant walked in, the professor handed her the letter. "This needs to be hand-delivered," he said, his tone filled with both determination and anxiety. This was his chance to make his dreams a reality, and he wasn't going to let anything stand in his way.

Pattie could sense the gravity of the situation as she took the letter from him. She knew how much this meant to him, how much time and effort he had put into this project. She couldn't help but feel a sense of admiration for her boss, his passion for archaeology and his unwavering determination.

Dr. Spigelman watched as she left the room, his mind racing with a mix of excitement and nervousness. The map from his dreams and the blackboard was his only clue, and he couldn't shake off the feeling that it was all leading to something big. But just as quickly as the thought came, he pushed it away and wadded up the map, throwing it into the trash. He couldn't let himself get distracted. He had work to do.

CHAPTER 24

PROFESSOR GEFEN INVESTIGATES

Arie Gefen was a man of many talents, but it was his photographic memory that set him apart from the rest. Few knew about this incredible ability of his, and he liked to keep it that way. It had served him well throughout his career as a scholar, collector, and gambler. He reveled in his uncanny knack for discerning undervalued treasures, instinctively capitalizing on opportune moments for his own advantage. But when he saw the family tree document with the name Simon of Cyrene at the end, his interest was immediately piqued.

Arie could still recall every detail of the document in his mind, as clearly as if it were laid out in front of him. The biblical significance of this name surfaced in his memory, sending a chill down his spine. This was a person mentioned in the Bible only once, on the day of the crucifixion. He had carried the cross of Jesus, and then he disappeared from history. What were the odds that his name would resurface over two thousand years later, with a personal message hidden within the document? "I must authenticate this document if it's the last thing I do," Arie declared, his voice filled with determination.

He sat down and began making a short list of colleagues he could trust with this sensitive information. Arie's keen sense of judgment and his total recall memory were a powerful combination, but they could not predict the doom that the name "Simon of Cyrene" would bring to his door. As he walked into the meeting room, located on the ground floor of his apartment complex, Arie was greeted by two familiar faces. Steven Goldberg, a longtime associate, and Brian Stellar, a colleague from the university who specialized in computer technology.

The room was always empty, especially in the middle of the day. Arie's mind was racing as he took his seat. He couldn't shake off the feeling of unease that had settled in his gut. He knew he was about to embark on a journey that would test his limits and push him to his breaking point. But he couldn't resist the call of the unknown and the promise of uncovering a hidden truth. Little did he know, the journey ahead would not only challenge his memory and judgment but also his very existence.

As the pieces of the puzzle began to fall into place, Arie would come face to face with his own demons and the consequences of his actions. But that was a story for another time. For now, as Arie delved deeper into the mystery of the family tree document, he had no idea what was about to unfold. The world as he knew it would never be the same again.

It was a picturesque scene, the large picture window casting a warm glow over the room, overlooking a serene duck pond that glistened in the sunlight. The outside swimming pool and deck added to the luxurious atmosphere of the place.

Steven, the man sitting in the room, was unassuming at first glance. But behind his thick glasses, there was a sharp intellect and a fierce determination. He rode his bike everywhere, never stopping in his pursuit of knowledge. Disappointments in his love life never discouraged him, and he continued to try. His expertise in biblical history was unmatched, and he had earned numerous awards for his extensive research and publications. His latest book, AD What Really Happened, had caused quite a stir in the academic world. But his most notable work was a deep investigation into the lives of the People Mentioned in the Bible. Some called him a modern day Sadducee, due to his beliefs that aligned with theirs a denial of life after death and the resurrection of Jesus.

Brian, on the other hand, was a contrast to Steven in every way. He was short and stocky, with a rugged build that hinted at his love for working out. He always had a Dr. Pepper in his hand, fueling his energy as he delved into his computer screen. Brian was a computer junkie, and his skills were unrivaled. He had helped Professor Gefen on numerous research projects, using his computer wizardry to crack codes, uncover hidden clues, and dig deeper than anyone could imagine.

Arie, a colleague of Steven and Brian, once remarked that if he had to choose between a historian and Brian, he would choose Brian every time. His ability to gather vast amounts of information in a matter of minutes and use it to solve problems was unparalleled. Arie, the man who had summoned Steven and Brian, pulled up a chair with a stunning view of the duck pond in the background. He was a man of mystery, with a sharp mind and a wealth of knowledge. He spoke with a voice that commanded attention, and his presence was felt by all those around him.

"I think you two know each other, don't you?" he asked, already knowing the answer. "Yes," replied Steven, "Brian and I have been acquainted for over a year now. We were just discussing that before you arrived." Arie smiled, his eyes sparkling with excitement. "Oh, yes...sorry I'm a few minutes late. I had a phone call I couldn't miss. But I'm glad you both could make it." "Not that we don't enjoy your company," interjected Brian, "but why exactly are we here?" Arie's expression turned serious. "I'll get straight to the point. Something strange has appeared on the radar screen...but it might not be anything." Steven furrowed his brow, his curiosity piqued. "What radar screen? I know nothing about airplanes." Arie chuckled. "No, not a real radar. Let's just say something has caught my attention, and it looks out of place. But it could be nothing." As Arie's words hung in the air, a sense of foreboding settled over the room.

The three men shared a knowing look, each bracing themselves for what was to come. As Arie spoke, his voice grew louder and more animated, his hands gesturing wildly as he explained the significance of the document. Steven and Brian leaned in closer, their eyes following his every move. "I could feel the weight of history in that room," Arie continued, his voice now tinged with excitement. "The document was old, I could tell just by looking at it. And the inscription, written in Hebrew, was like a secret code waiting to be deciphered." Steven's brow furrowed in confusion. "But who is this Simon of Cyrene? I've never heard of him before." Arie's eyes sparkled as he answered. "He's not just a character in a story; he's a real person. And according to this document, he has a direct connection to the crucifixion of Jesus." Brian's interest was piqued. "But how is that possible? I thought the only people involved in the crucifixion were Jesus and the disciples." Arie's grin widened. "That's what makes this so intriguing. The inscription was a message from Alexander, one of Simon's sons. And let me tell you, it's not just any message." Steven leaned forward, his curiosity now fully awakened. "What did it say?" Arie's voice grew hushed and reverent, his eyes wide and his hands trembling slightly. "It was a personal message, written by hand, from Alexander to his ancestor, the Professor." Arie's voice cracked with emotion as he continued, "But you will need to wait to hear what it says."

The three men sat in stunned silence, their minds racing with the implications of this discovery. Arie's eyes were filled with wonder and awe, his voice filled with reverence as he spoke of the ancient message. Brian, usually the emotional one, was visibly moved, his eyes glistening with unshed tears. As the weight of this circumstance sank in, the air around them seemed to grow heavier, the room becoming charged with a sense of history and mystery. The very air seemed to hum with the energy of the past, and the three men could feel themselves being pulled into the story of Alexander and the Professor.

Arie's voice took on a new depth, his words resonating with the weight of centuries. "Can you imagine?" he said, his eyes shining with excitement. "A message from a 2000-year-old person to a future relative, preserved for centuries, hidden under a seemingly ordinary family tree." As he spoke, the room seemed to fade away, and the men were transported back in time, feeling the weight of the message and the connection between past, present, and future. Brian and Steven were both captivated by Arie's words, their minds racing with the possibilities of what this message could contain.

"It's like we're getting a glimpse into the lives of these people, into their hearts and souls." Steven nodded. "And the fact that it's connected to the crucifixion, to Jesus himself, makes it all the more powerful."

Arie smiled, his voice now gentle and filled with wonder. "I think this document has the power to change everything we thought we knew about that day, about those people. They knew that this discovery would change their lives forever. And as they left the room, they couldn't help but feel that they had just been a part of something truly extraordinary.

"What did the message say?" Steven asked, his eyes boring into Arie's with the intensity of a hungry predator. Arie's lip curled into a sly grin as he leaned in, his voice dropping to a low, conspiratorial tone. "Like this wasn't intriguing enough, the message started out by saying, 'My distant brother.' Can you imagine? He knew exactly who he was writing to, two thousand years in the future. A personal message, just for us." Steven's eyes widened in disbelief, while Brian leaned in closer, his interest piqued. "And then what?" he prodded, unable to contain his curiosity. Arie's grin widened. "Oh, it gets better. The message goes on to say, 'My name is Alexander.' He identifies himself, right off the bat." Steven's jaw dropped, while Brian let out a low whistle. "But why would someone linked to the crucifixion, named Alexander, leave a message for an archaeologist with the same name, two thousand years later?" Brian mused. Arie's eyes sparkled with excitement. "Who knows? But it gets even more intriguing. He not only declares himself as Alexander, but also as 'son of Simon of Cyrene and brother to Rufus.' Can you imagine the implications of that?" Steven and Brian exchanged stunned looks, before turning back to Arie. "What does it all mean?" Steven asked, barely able to contain his excitement. Arie shrugged, a mischievous glint in his eye. "I'm not sure, but there's more. He finishes the message with, and get this, 'I have something to tell you.' Can you imagine the secrets this Alexander is about to reveal?"

The three men sat in stunned silence, their minds reeling with the possibilities. The air around them seemed to crackle with energy, as they waited with bated breath for Arie to continue. "Are you kidding me?" Brian finally exclaimed, breaking the silence. "This is unbelievable." Arie's grin widened into a full-fledged smile. "Believe it, my friends. We're on the brink of uncovering a mystery that's been hidden for over two thousand years. And we have a very important message waiting for us. Now I don't know about you," Arie said, leaning closer to Steven and Brian, "but that sounds like someone is a time traveler." "No, way," Brian exclaimed, his eyes wide with excitement. "This is getting deep." Steven nodded in agreement, his mind racing with possibilities. "So the message reads, 'My name is Alexander, son of Simon of Cyrene and brother to Rufus. I have something to tell you.' Is that right?" Arie confirmed, handing each of them a folder. "I've taken the liberty to outline some key points we need to investigate," he continued, his voice low and intense. "You are both in on this, aren't you?" Steven and Brian exchanged a knowing glance before opening their folders. "Where do we start?" Steven asked, eager to dive into the mysterious message. "You will see as we move along that I've divided tasks into areas of expertise," Arie explained. "First my task: The age of the document—I will need Debi for this. I will see if we can somehow examine the original."

A sense of urgency filled the room as Arie continued, "I will examine the Hebrew letters to see if I can determine what time period the author of the message lived. We must know the truth, no matter how impossible it may seem." Steven and Brian nodded in agreement, ready to do whatever it takes to unravel the mystery. "These tasks are for Steven," Arie instructed, his voice growing even more intense.

"Look into the existence of Simon of Cyrene; look deep into cults that may have developed around his life and passed down information and secrets, folklore, or anything to go on. We need to know what happened to Simon after he carried the cross of Jesus." Steven's mind raced with possibilities as he began to formulate a plan. "No one ever considered that his name would surface two thousand years later, so no one cared what happened to him.

We need to find out." Arie turned to Brian, his eyes burning with determination. "Look deep in the underworld for any information on Alexander and Rufus. Did they ever mention their father Simon in a way that got recorded and documented? If so, we need to find it and see what they said." Somewhere in the shadows, Arie whispered, "The truth lies within the darkness." he continued, "Brian: We need to find any mention, no matter how small of Simon of Cyrene, Alexander, or Rufus that might be in the cloud. Anything that might lead us to someone who has information about the existence of Simon or Alexander." Brian nodded, his eyes scanning the information in his folder.

"I will do whatever it takes to uncover the truth." Arie's voice grew even more intense as he turned again to Steven, "We need for you to continue to trace the lineage of this … uh … Dr. Alexander Spigelman back to Simon. I will provide you with a detailed list of names that connect Spigelman with Simon; you will be able to start there." Steven's heart raced with anticipation. This was the breakthrough they had been waiting for. Arie concluded, "This will be like finding a needle in a haystack, but if it is out there, we need to find it."

The three of them sat in silence, each lost in their own thoughts, determined to uncover the truth no matter what it takes.

CHAPTER 25

THE VOICE IS REVEALED

Dr Spigelman's feet pounded against the pavement as he ran through the quiet streets this morning. He felt more alive than ever before. His heart raced with excitement, for today was the day he would find out which site had been approved for his archaeological expedition to Jerusalem. A weight had been lifted off his shoulders when his funding request was approved, and now he was filled with an uncommonly good mood. As he looked into the mirror in his bathroom, he couldn't help but smile at the reflection staring back at him. Alexander Spigelman, about to embark on the adventure of a lifetime. His father would be proud.

He gathered his briefcase and headed to work, eagerly anticipating what the day would bring. Pattie, his assistant, greeted him with her usual warm smile. As he hung up his jacket, he couldn't help but notice the beautiful flowers on her desk. The scent of them filled the air, adding to the already beautiful day. "What a beautiful day this is," Pattie exclaimed. "Did you have a good run this morning?" she asked, noticing the pep in his step. "Why yes," the professor replied. "Do you like the flowers I sent you?" he joked. Pattie's smile faltered for a moment before she explained, "You didn't send them...they're from my husband. It's our anniversary."

"Oh, I'm sorry, Pattie," he said apologetically. "I didn't have it written down on my calendar, or I would have gotten you something. I tell you what, take the rest of the day off and let me treat you to some relaxation. How about a facial and a pedicure?" Pattie's face lit up with gratitude. "That is so sweet of you, Professor, but a facial...do you think I need one?" He instantly regretted his words. "Oh, no," he backtracked. "You are beautiful for your age." But his foot kept getting deeper and deeper as he tried to save himself from his earlier blunder. He mentally cursed himself for his lack of tact.

As a renowned professor and director of an excavation site, he should have been more careful with his words. But in that moment, he was just a man, trying to make amends for his mistake. "You know what I mean," he growled, his voice dripping with frustration. Pattie could see the tension in his jaw as he clenched it tightly. "Yes, I do," she replied calmly, trying not to provoke him further. But she couldn't help the small smirk that played on her lips.

She knew how easily he could get worked up, especially when it came to his work. "I'll let you off the hook this time," she said, her eyes twinkling mischievously. "But only because I don't want you to choke on your own foot." She handed him a letter, her laughter ringing through the room. "It came this morning, hand delivered. Looks like it's your site approval." He took the letter from her, his hand trembling slightly. "I know," he said, his voice barely above a whisper. But his excitement quickly turned to confusion as he read the letter. Pattie could see the emotions playing across his face, exhilaration, befuddlement, and finally, anger. "Did your site get approved?" she asked, her tone filled with concern. "Yes...

no...I mean, a site I did get approved. But I never requested it," he said, his voice rising in frustration. He frantically searched through his wastebasket, muttering to himself. "Where is it? Where did it go?" Pattie watched him, her curiosity piqued. "What are you looking for?" "The paper you brought me the other day. The one from the unknown student," he said, his voice laced with urgency. "I need to see it again." Pattie's eyes widened in understanding. She remembered the strange document he had received, and the bizarre events that had followed. "I remember," she said cautiously. "But what does that have to do with anything?" "Here it is," he exclaimed triumphantly, pulling out a crumpled piece of paper from the wastebasket. "Thank goodness housekeeping never empties this thing." He unfolded the paper, his eyes scanning it frantically. "I've been experiencing some weird things ever since this showed up," he said, his voice trembling with unease. "I've been seeing and hearing things that can't possibly be real. Someone or something is messing with my mind." Pattie's heart raced as she listened to him. "What do you mean? What kind of things?" His eyes met hers, and for a moment, she saw fear in them. "I don't know. But I have a feeling it's only just begun." "Like what?" asked Pattie, her voice tinged with confusion. She furrowed her brows, her eyes darting between the professor and the mysterious folder in his hand.

"Well, the other day as I was trying to decide which sites to request, you brought me this folder from the unknown student. Inside was a drawing of a map with instructions to dig in a particular location. I wadded it up and threw it in the trash; you saw me retrieve it. This is the site that got approved; I didn't even have it listed as an option." Pattie's heart began to race as she processed the professor's words. Her mind was filled with a flurry of questions and suspicions. Who was this unknown student? Why did they want to dig in that specific location? exclaimed Pattie, her voice trembling with disbelief. Her mind was racing, trying to make sense of the strange turn of events. "What do you make of it?" asked the professor, his voice heavy with uncertainty. Pattie's lips parted in shock, unable to form a coherent response. She shook her head, her mind unable to wrap around the bizarre and unnerving possibility that someone from beyond the grave was trying to make contact. "My mother said she saw my grandmother cooking in the kitchen one day after she passed away," offered Pattie, her voice laced with a mix of fear and fascination. "Maybe someone close to you wants to have closure." The professor's eyes widened in surprise, his mind racing with possibilities. Could it be? Was someone trying to reach out to him from beyond the grave? The thought sent shivers down his spine. "Thanks, Pattie, I'm sure that is it," he said, his voice barely above a whisper.

"You better hurry, or your day off will be gone." "Thanks, Dr. Spigelman", she said, her voice filled with a mix of determination and unease as she closed the office door behind her. Dr. Spigelman was now deeply troubled. No matter what he did, he could not shake off the haunting voice that had been plaguing him. And now, it was actively sabotaging his efforts to dig in a legitimate location. The worst part was that it was now too late to submit another site. The professor let out a heavy sigh, his mind consumed with fear and uncertainty. Something was not right, and he couldn't shake off the feeling that he was being watched. He couldn't escape the thought that someone or something was trying to communicate with him, and it was now up to him to uncover the truth.

The voice wins. The professor stayed in his office after Pattie left, the weight of the situation pressing down on him. He began to research the latitude, longitude, and topography of the secluded and untouched area surrounding the dig site. The approval letter came as a surprise, its tone almost disbelieving that anyone would want to venture there. But it was perfect for what the voice wanted. "Why do you want me to dig there?" he asked out loud, his voice trembling with both fear and curiosity.

There was a pause before the voice responded, its tone both haunting and commanding. "So, do you believe I'm real?" Spigelman almost jumped out of his shoes at the sound of the voice, his heart racing in his chest. "Jesus," he gasped, "do you have to do that?" "Do you have to use the name of Jesus like that?" the voice retorted, its tone filled with sorrow and disappointment. "He was real, you know, and he paid a painful price for you." "I know, I know," Spigelman stammered, "but I'm not sure what I believe. Why did you switch my locations? Is there something you want me to find?" "I told you before, if you believe me, I can share more with you," the voice replied, its tone growing more urgent, "but this situation has now become extremely volatile and could turn violent. The less you know, the safer you are right now." "Don't leave me hanging like this," Spigelman pleaded, his mind racing with questions and confusion. "You are the one who came to me, remember?"

"Okay," the voice said, its tone softening slightly, "I'm going to try and reveal myself to you, but this all depends on you. You must stay focused and remember, you can only see what you believe." "This reminds me of Dorothy and the Wizard of Oz," the professor rambled on, his mind grasping at any semblance of normalcy. "Do I need to click my heels together three times?" "What are you talking about?" the voice asked, its confusion evident. In that moment, Spigelman realized that he was in a completely different world, one where anything was possible and nothing was as it seemed. He took a deep breath and braced himself for whatever was to come, knowing that he was no longer in control of his own fate"Please sit down; I can sense the tension emanating from you," the professor's voice rang out, thick with concern. He made his way over to his desk, the weight of his years evident in every step.

Just then, a shadow flickered on the other side of the room, causing the hairs on the back of his neck to stand on end. The thought of "beam me up, Scotty" flashed through his mind as the figure faded in and out of existence. It was like nothing he had ever experienced before. "Do you believe I'm here?" the voice asked, its tone filled with an otherworldly quality. The professor's heart raced as he struggled to find the words to respond. "Yes, I believe. How could I not?" he finally managed to say, his voice trembling. As he spoke those words, the figure solidified in front of him, revealing himself to be a young man. "My name is Alexander Spiegel," the young man said, his voice carrying a depth and wisdom far beyond his years. "You can call me Alex."

The professor's mind reeled at the realization that this young man, who appeared to be no more than a boy, was from a time long past. "My name is Dr. Alexander Spigelman, and you can call me Professor," he replied, still trying to process the situation. "But how is this possible? You seem so young. Where did you come from?" Alex's eyes seemed to hold a thousand stories as he explained, "My spirit has traveled through time to reach you. My body is still in the past, hidden away in a cave - a cave that God provided for King David to hide in many years before my time. I come from a time just after the crucifixion of Jesus." The professor's mind spun with disbelief.

"Wait, you mean to tell me that your body is lying in a cave where King David once sought refuge, and you have witnessed the crucifixion of Jesus?" he asked, his voice tinged with awe. Alex simply nodded in response. The professor couldn't help but feel like he was living in a storybook. "Where is this cave?" he inquired, his curiosity piqued. "I do not know the exact location, only that it is somewhere in the desert. But that is not important," Alex replied. "What is important is that you follow through with the dig at that location. Trust me, it will lead to a life-changing discovery." And just like that, Alex was gone, leaving the professor to process everything he had just heard.

As any good teacher would, the professor reached for a folder in his desk and began jotting down notes while they were fresh in his mind. As he studied the family tree once again, a realization dawned on him - Alexander was a distant ancestor. The young man who had just been standing in his office was his own distant grandfather. The thought left him reeling, but he knew he had work to do. With a renewed sense of purpose, the professor left his office to prepare for the dig. This was a once-in-a-lifetime opportunity, and he was determined to make the most of it.

CHAPTER 26

DEBI TAKES THE DOCUMENT

It was a dreary and dismal day, with thick clouds blanketing the sky and a forecast predicting light snowfall later in the afternoon. Debi despised these types of days, knowing they often meant a slow and uneventful day at work. She stood at the large front window, gazing out with a wistful look in her eye, daydreaming of warm summer days, crystal clear oceans, luxurious cruises, and a candlelit Dinner. But her reverie was interrupted as she noticed Arie approaching. She couldn't help but wonder what he wanted from her.

Quickly, she began to busy herself with work as Arie made his way to her desk. Debi looked up, flashing a seductive smile that she knew had a way of melting men in their tracks. She had learned to use this to her advantage at a young age, and it had proven effective in many situations. "Hi, Arie," she purred. "To what do I owe this pleasure?" She couldn't help but think, please don't tell me you're expecting homemade cookies. "I need to ask a favor from you," Arie replied, his tone dripping with a hint of mischief. "You know, payback for all the times I've helped you out." Debi raised an eyebrow, feigning surprise. "What on earth could I do for you?" she asked. Then, with a sly smile, she added, "Actually, let me rephrase that: What could I do that wouldn't get us both in trouble?" Arie chuckled, his charming smile lighting up his face.

Debi couldn't help but think that someday someone needed to put a leash on him. "You remember that document your friend Pattie asked your help with?" Arie began. Debi nodded, remembering the mysterious document from Dr. Spigelman that Pattie had been investigating. "Well, I was wondering if I could take a look at the original," Arie continued, his eyes sparkling with curiosity. Debi knew better than to trust Arie's seemingly innocent request. She knew that if he wanted a second look at something, there was something in it for him. Or he believed there was a lot of money to be made.

"What's in it for you?" she asked, getting straight to the point. Arie leaned in, his voice low and conspiratorial. "As I told you the other day, if this document is authentic, it could date all the way back to the time of the crucifixion. And my dear lady, that would make it a huge story." Debi's interest was piqued. But she also knew that there was more to this than just a potential groundbreaking story. "No, there's more to this than just a story," she said, her voice filled with determination. "Let me in on what's really going on, and I'll get you the document to examine." "Okay, I knew you wouldn't be easily persuaded," Arie's voice was thick with frustration as he paced back and forth in front of Debi's desk.

"So, I prepared a summary of what the importance of this discovery might hold if we can authenticate the family tree. Read over it and let me know." His piercing gaze bore into her, as if daring her to reject his offer. Debi couldn't help but feel a twinge of annoyance at his persistence. She had known Arie for years, and while he was undeniably brilliant, he could also be quite pushy when he wanted something. But she couldn't deny the excitement that bubbled up inside her at the thought of uncovering something truly significant. As Arie turned to walk out of the door, he couldn't resist taking one last jab at Debi. "By the way, the answer to what you can do-" he let the sentence trail off, a sly smile playing at the corners of his mouth. But Debi didn't take the bait. Instead, she simply raised an eyebrow and replied, "Save it and get out of here before I call security and tell them you tried to undress me. "But I did," Arie insisted. "I know," Debi replied, her eyes sparkling with mischief. "You can leave that image here, so you don't have a heart attack going home."

As the slow day dragged on, Debi took the opportunity to carefully review what Arie had left for her. She couldn't deny the uniqueness of a handwritten message from someone two thousand years ago to what appeared to be the intended recipient. And the more she delved into the message, the more she began to realize the gravity of its contents. "I have something to tell you," Debi read aloud, her voice filled with wonder. It was clear that the sender wanted a current physical meeting to share something important. But that couldn't be possible, could it? Her mind whirled with questions, and she couldn't help but feel a sense of unease about the mysterious disappearance of Simon after he was mentioned in the Bible. It was almost as if he had fallen off the map, never to be heard from again. No wonder people said he never existed.

But if this document was true, it meant that not only did Simon exist, but his son Alexander had somehow managed to travel through time to bring a message to the world. It was a thought too incredible to comprehend, yet Debi couldn't deny the overwhelming sense of excitement and curiosity that coursed through her veins.

Without hesitation, she picked up the phone and called Arie. "I was expecting your call," he said, his voice laced with satisfaction. "I'm in. I'll let you know when I get the document." Debi couldn't wait to see what secrets and mysteries awaited her within its pages.

Debi started to call Pattie, but realized it was her anniversary and that she had taken the afternoon off. Debi remembered that she had asked Pattie if Professor Spigelman ever finished looking into his genealogy, and she said she didn't know, that he didn't talk about it. But he kept the folder handy, in his top desk drawer, and would probably investigate it more after the dig. Debi picked up the phone and called Dr. Spigelman's office, but no one answered. The voice mail picked up with an out-of-office message from Dr. Spigelman saying, "I'm out of the office, please leave a message." That was all Debi needed to hear; she knew there was no better time than today to swap out the documents. I am an expert at forging old documents, and Dr. Spigelman is not interested in the age of the document. He is just interested in the family tree and the lineage on the document. He will never know they have been swapped.

Debi knocked on Professor Spigelman's door, but as expected, no one answered. She quickly entered and closed the door behind her. She made her way into his office and shut and locked the door behind her. "Now," she said, "where is the folder? ... In the top drawer ... right or left? I have a 50-50 chance of getting it right the first time," she said. "Here we go, that was easy. I'll have this folder back before anyone knows. ... Wait just a minute, what is this? Looks like the professor has already met our stranger from the past, and he took notes. These notes are for my eyes only," she whispered as she left the office.

CHAPTER 27

LUCIFER HEARS THE NAME "SIMON"

Steven was meeting with Adam Stuart, a longtime colleague of his but one he had not seen for a while. The two had collaborated on some research into ancient religion many years ago, but their friendship had been strained by their conflicting beliefs. Adam was a priest in an underground church, the leader of a clandestine community that worshipped "Lucifer god of earth." Steven had always been fascinated by Adam's mysterious ways, but he never imagined he would have to enter the underground world himself.

As Steven made his way through the dark, damp corridors, his heart raced with a mixture of fear and excitement. He had been instructed to meet with Adam in secret, and he had no idea what to expect. But as he approached the designated meeting spot, he encountered a shady figure on the street corner. The man had no face, his head covered by a hoodie and his eyes hidden behind sunglasses, even though the sun had long set. Steven was instructed to get into a waiting vehicle, its windows darkened to conceal their identities. He was then blindfolded and driven for what felt like an eternity.

When the vehicle finally came to a stop, the blindfold was taken off, he was led out and into what seemed like a cave. The air was thick with the smell of damp earth, and the only sound was the echoing of voices. As he was led deeper into the cave, Steven's senses were bombarded with sights and sounds that he had never experienced before. Torches lined the walls, casting flickering shadows that danced around him. The air was considerably colder and draftier than he had anticipated, and he couldn't help but shiver as he followed his mysterious guide.

Finally, they arrived at a giant chamber that seemed to be set up for sacrifice and ceremonies. At the head of the room sat a prodigious throne, and at its base was a table shaped like a pentagram. It was clear that this was a place of worship, but not to any god that Steven was familiar with. He was instructed to sit and wait, and as the minutes ticked by, he couldn't help but feel a sense of unease. His unease turned to fear when he noticed a blood-stained altar in the corner of the room, elevated higher than the pentagram table. Strange symbols adorned its surface, and Steven couldn't help but feel a sense of dread wash over him. He had never encountered anything like this before, and he couldn't shake the feeling that he was in way over his head.

Just when he was considering making a run for it, a voice broke the silence. "I hope you haven't been waiting long," it said, causing Steven to nearly jump out of his skin. It was Adam, and he was standing right in front of him, his eyes glinting in the torchlight. "Jesus, Adam, don't do that," Steven exclaimed, forgetting where he was for a moment. But Adam's reaction was swift and fierce. He covered his ears and demanded that Steven never use that name again. Steven realized with a jolt that he had just committed a grave mistake. In this underground world, the name of Jesus was forbidden, and he had just broken one of their most sacred rules.

Suddenly, he couldn't wait to get out of there and back to the safety of the world above. The hairs on the back of Steven's neck stood up as he stared into Adam's eyes. They seemed to glow with an intense, fiery light, sending shivers down his spine. He could practically feel the heat radiating off him as he sat on the imposing throne, his presence filling the room. Steven couldn't help but feel a twinge of fear as he looked at the powerful demon before him. How had he managed to sneak up on him without him noticing? It was as if Adam had appeared out of thin air, using some sort of dark magic to cloak his movements. As Adam laughed and leaned down to look at him, Steven couldn't help but feel a sense of unease. There was something off about this creature, something that made him uneasy in his presence.

But he couldn't let that stop him. He had a mission to complete, and he couldn't let fear get in the way. So, he squared his shoulders and met Adam's intense gaze, determined to get the answers he needed. "I've heard a name," Steven began, his voice steady despite the tremor in his hands. "Simon of Cyrene. Does that name mean anything to you?" Adam's laughter abruptly stopped, and his expression turned serious. He seemed to grow larger, his body shifting and contorting until he was a monstrous werewolf, towering over Steven with razor-sharp teeth and claws that could tear him apart in an instant. Steven's heart pounded in his chest as the temperature in the room dropped, a cold chill settling in the air. He couldn't believe what he was seeing, couldn't believe that this creature was the same person he had just been speaking to.

But he couldn't back down now. He had come this far, and he needed to know the truth. "I-I heard it in a prophecy," Steven stammered, his voice trembling. "A prophecy about the end of days. They say you hold the key to unlocking it." Adam's eyes blazed with an otherworldly light, and Steven could feel the raw power emanating from him. He was both terrified and fascinated by this creature before him, wondering what secrets he held and what darkness lurked within him. But before he could say anything else, Adam let out an ear-splitting roar and lunged at him, his claws reaching for his throat. Steven cowered in fear, knowing that he was no match for this monstrous being.

In that moment, he realized that he was truly in Satan's country, facing a creature straight out of his worst nightmares. And he could only hope that he would make it out alive. "I will tell you..." Steven's voice trembled as he spoke, fear dripping from every word. "I will tell you... just don't hurt me. Please don't hurt me – it means nothing to me." The werewolf paced around Steven, sniffing at him with a menacing glare from its glowing eyes. "I have not heard that name for centuries on top of centuries," it growled. "You have recently been around Arie, haven't you? I will never forget his smell, but there is a new smell, one I don't know. Who is it?" Its voice was deep and commanding, sending shivers down Steven's spine. "It is Brian..." Steven stammered, his heart racing in fear. "Brian... I can't remember his last name." The werewolf's growl intensified, its patience running thin. "Tell me," it roared, baring its sharp teeth. "Or I will have you for dinner." "Brian Stellar," Steven blurted out, his voice trembling. "He is a computer specialist who has worked with Arie on other projects before." The werewolf's eyes narrowed, as if trying to place the name. "What is your business asking about Simon of Cyrene?" it demanded, its voice echoing through the dark forest. "Arie ran across a family tree document of a local professor, uh... Dr. Spigelman, Alexander Spigelman," Steven explained, his voice shaking. "His lineage went all the way back to Simon of Cyrene. But that can't be true, right? Simon isn't a real person... so the document must be fake. I'll go and tell Arie, I swear."

His words trailed off as the werewolf's eyes bore into his own. But the werewolf didn't seem convinced. "Simon of Cyrene," it repeated, its voice low and menacing. "A name I haven't heard in a long time. And yet, this document... it must be real. Why else would Arie be looking into it?" Its voice grew more and more agitated, its grip on Steven tightening. Steven's heart pounded in his chest as he tried to think of a way out. He couldn't betray Arie, but he also couldn't risk his own life. "I don't know anything else," he whimpered. "I swear, that's all I know." The werewolf's grip loosened slightly, but its eyes still burned with intensity. "You better be telling the truth," it growled. "Because if I find out you're lying..." Its threat hung in the air, unspoken but heavily implied. Steven took a deep breath, trying to calm his racing heart. He knew he had to be careful from now on. The werewolf may have let him go for now, but he couldn't trust it to keep its word. Not when it came to something as important as the mysterious Simon of Cyrene.

"Why is Arie so fascinated by this document?" the demon asks Steven, his voice dripping with curiosity and malice. "Is it the promise of fame and fortune that drives him?" The demon's words hung in the air, sending chills down Steven's spine. And as the demon continued to prod and manipulate, the stakes only grew higher, igniting a firestorm of passion and turmoil. Upon asking that, the werewolf couldn't contain his anger anymore and slashed Steven's arm off at the shoulder. Steven lay screaming in agony as blood spurted everywhere. "I can stop the bleeding if you tell me who else knows about this," the demon said. "Just me, Brian, and Arie—and a lady named Debi at the genealogy department. Please, can you save me now?" begged Steven. "Can you stop the bleeding? I'm getting weak." "Yes, take my hand and stand up," Adam said, reaching down to offer a helping hand. But when Steven made it to his feet, Adam sliced his other arm off and looked into Steven's eyes when he said, "But I won't." Then he chopped Steven's head off and watched his body jerk and shake on the floor.

CHAPTER 28

THE DOCUMENT IS STOLEN

Debi took the folder back to her office, which was about a fifteen-minute walk-through campus or a three-minute drive (plus a fifteen-minute search to find a parking place). Most days, Debi enjoyed walking if her destination was on campus, because she enjoyed the attention she got from the young college guys. Today, however, it was late in the afternoon, and not many students were out walking. The weather was cold, and snow flurries were starting to fall, so she drove to Professor Spigelman's office. "I must get this folder back to his office before anyone finds out," she said as she was pulling into an almost empty parking lot at her office building. The wind suddenly picked up, making it hard to open the car door. As she struggled to open the door against the brisk wind, a polite gentleman came from nowhere and opened it for her. Debi was startled and caught off guard; she had just pulled into an empty parking lot where she always looked around for strangers before getting out of her car. No one was around.

She had no time to react, but she was wondering where this guy came from. Debi was a good judge of character and could size someone up quickly—and she was almost always right. But for some reason, she couldn't penetrate this guy. He was an elegant looking man, tall, well groomed, and polite; he wore extremely expensive jewelry. My kind of guy, Debi thought, as she melted when her eyes met his. "Allow me. My name is Adam. Your wish is my command, pretty lady," he said. Now that sent thoughts racing through Debi's mind that almost short-circuited her speech process. She was having a hard time smiling, talking, or doing anything but staring. "What is your name, my beautiful princess?" Adam asked, using all the right words to flatter her. Debi stepped from her car while holding Adam's hand for assistance. "My name is Debi ... where in the world did you come from?" she asked. "It's magic," Adam said, "done with lights and mirrors," followed with a laugh that was a little unnerving. Just then a stiff breeze hit Debi in the face, and she realized the temperature must have dropped fifteen degrees in the last few minutes. "May I help you to the building with your briefcase and papers?" Adam offered. "The wind is whipping, and if you drop your papers, you may never find them all." "No, thanks," responded Debi. "I can make it fine, and thanks for opening the car door." "My pleasure," said Adam with a smile. "Maybe we will see each other again." "Yes, maybe," said Debi, but by now her radar was saying, no—stay away from this guy.

Debi started towards the building, but out of instinct glanced back over her shoulder, and as quickly as Adam had appeared, he'd disappeared. He was nowhere in sight, and he didn't leave in a vehicle or on a bike. That was strange, she thought as she walked toward the front door, the temperature just warmed back up. Debi got to her office and was visibly shaken. What started out to be a pleasant surprise—a good-looking stranger stepping out of the edges of darkness to offer assistance—ended up creeping her out. She took a moment and got a cup of hot coffee, which was good and strong because it had been brewing all afternoon. She turned the coffeepot off and returned to her desk.

Now, she thought, I can get to work. Debi reached for her stack of papers, looking for the folder from Dr. Spigelman's desk. She casually shuffled through the stack to find the one she was searching for. When she didn't see it right off, she franticly dug deeper through the stack; it wasn't there. Debi opened her briefcase and looked inside, even though she knew she hadn't put the folder there. She quickly retraced her steps back to her car when it dawned on her, "I handed the stranger my papers as I got out of the car." Panic was starting to creep in. "Think, Debi, think." He held my papers and gave me a hand getting out of the car but handed the papers back to me as soon as I got out. How could he take the folder without me seeing and where did he put it? she wondered. She then remembered that Adam came and went as the wind, here one minute and gone the next; he was no ordinary person.

Debi returned to her desk where reality started sinking in—she had been taken. Adam had stolen the folder, and the information contained in the folder was more dangerous than anyone knew. Debi grabbed the copy she had and got busy forging a replacement to take back to Dr. Spigelman's office. At this point, Debi was not concerned about the professor, but she would hate for her friend Pattie to find out that she'd had anything to do with the document going missing. Debi remembered the notes placed on the outside of the folder and forged them, word for word, so the folder looked exactly like the one taken. If she didn't know better, she would think it was the same folder. Debi rushed the folder back to the office ... then called Arie and set up a meeting for the next morning.

* * * *

EVIL DECEPTION

The next day, when Arie got to the coffee shop, Debi was already there. Arie looked worried as he approached Debi's table ... looking over his shoulder several times as he sat down. Arie is not his cocky self, thought Debi. He didn't smile ... didn't comment on my hair, and didn't even look like he was undressing me with his eyes. "What is this all about?" said Arie. "Well, good morning to you too," said Debi. "What is wrong with you, Arie? You seem on edge like I've never seen you before." "I'm worried," he said. "Steven was looking into the underworld cults, and I haven't been able to reach him for two days now." "Steven? Was he someone helping with this investigation?" asked Debi. "Yes, and when I talked to him last, he was meeting with an old associate of his who dealt in Satan worship. He was somewhat fearful but decided to go to the meeting anyway. He said the man's name was Adam." At the mention of the name Adam, Debi's face turned white as a sheet. She wanted to get up and leave but couldn't ... she wanted to run, but her feet and legs wouldn't move. She tried to speak, but nothing came out, her head started spinning ... The next thing she knew, Arie was washing her face with a cold rag, and the coffee shop staff were standing over her asking if she was all right. Someone asked if 911 should be called, but Arie said, "No, she is coming around now."

When she recovered, Arie asked, "What was that all about?" Debi stared off into space for a few minutes before she started to speak. "The reason I asked you to meet me here today is something strange, almost demonic happened last evening. I had just pulled into the almost empty parking lot at my office with the folder in hand. Right then the temperature dropped twenty degrees, and the wind picked up to the point I was having trouble opening the car door, and suddenly there stood a man. I always look when I pull into a parking lot to see who is around, for safety reasons you know. No one was there. This guy came from nowhere, I'm telling you. He opened my door and offered to help me out of the car. I said no, but he insisted. I handed him the stack of papers in my lap, and he gave me his hand and helped me to my feet. He then gave me back the papers." "What is strange about that?" asked Arie. "He said his name was Adam, and he stole the folder from me without me seeing him, even though he never left my sight.

Then he disappeared as quickly as he appeared," said Debi. "He stole the folder. How do you know it was him? Maybe you lost it or misplaced it, or—Debi stopped him in midsentence. "I looked everywhere. I've exhausted every possible reason, but it keeps coming back to this: I had it … he shows up … I don't have it." "Adam got the folder." "Arie, what do you make of this?" asked Debi. "I don't know, but we all could be in danger. We must drop this investigation immediately," said Arie. "I'll call Brian right now."

As he picked up his cell phone and punched speed dial, he added, "I don't think Brian has started his investigation yet." Arie's face turned white and fear gripped him by the throat when the voice that answered Brian's phone said, "Hello, Arie, this is Adam. Brian is unable to speak right now; he seems to have lost his head for the moment."

CHAPTER 29

WAR TWO THOUSAND YEARS IN THE FUTURE

Satan seethed with uncontrollable rage; his plan had been foiled once again, and his wrath knew no bounds. His infernal army trembled in fear as they spread the news of their master's fury. Even the most formidable demons cowered in terror, knowing the consequences of incurring Satan's wrath. In a fit of unbridled fury, Satan summoned all his top generals to his throne room. The ground shook and the skies turned blood red as they gathered before their enraged leader. Each demon could feel the searing heat emanating from Satan's fiery gaze, and their very souls quaked under his piercing stare. Whispers spread through the demon world as news of Satan's anger reached every corner. Some demons tried to flee, but there was no escaping the wrath of their master.

For they knew all too well what had happened the last time Satan was this furious. In a display of his power, Satan had destroyed his top demons before binding more of them, hand and foot and casting them into his own fiery furnace. The sound of their screams still echoed in the minds of those who had witnessed the horrific punishment. And now, with his fury unleashed once again, there was no telling what fate awaited his top generals.

Satan's voice boomed through the underworld, resonating with malice and hatred. His fiery eyes glinted with sadistic pleasure as he planned his revenge against those who had betrayed him. The air grew thick with tension, and even the bravest demons dared not make a sound in the presence of their furious master. For Satan was not just a ruler, he was a tyrant. A complex and intriguing character with a thirst for power and a penchant for destruction. And as the demon world trembled in fear, they knew that no one could escape the wrath of Satan.

Satan was in a terrifying state, his entire being aglow with an otherworldly inferno. Fire blazed from his eyes, nostrils, and mouth, igniting everything in its path. Lightning crackled and snaked from his fingertips, striking fear into the hearts of all who witnessed it. As the first ten demons dared to enter his chambers, they were met with a wrath unlike any they had ever experienced. In a blinding flash, they were engulfed in flames and hurled into the abyss, their agonized screams echoing throughout the underworld.

But it was not just his immense power and fury that made Satan so formidable. His presence alone was suffocating, a palpable weight that bore down on all those in his vicinity. His dark, twisted form exuded a malevolent energy that sent shivers down the spines of even the bravest souls. Truly, in that moment, Satan was a force to be reckoned with. A being of pure destruction and chaos, embodying all that is dark and sinister. And as he reveled in the chaos of his domain, his menacing laughter echoed through the halls, a chilling reminder of his ultimate control over the underworld.

Satan clenched the folder tightly in his hand, his eyes scanning the pages with disbelief. "Who dares to search for Simon of Cyrene?" he growled, his voice dripping with venom. "And why now, when I am about to expose the truth, well my truth anyway, about Jesus? A mere mortal, a fraud, a failure!" His rage intensified as he thought about the message Alexander had delivered to this human. "And what does Alexander know that I do not? The only way he could have traveled to the future is through divine intervention. This is the work of Michael!" Satan's voice thundered, echoing through the corridors of hell.

Frustrated, he slammed the folder onto his desk. "I must know what Alexander knows about Simon," he seethed. The thought of someone else having information that he did not was maddening. Satan paced back and forth, his mind racing with possibilities. He needed to get to the bottom of this, to unravel the mystery surrounding Simon of Cyrene. As he calmed down, a sly grin spread across his face. "Perhaps I can use this to my advantage," he chuckled, his dark eyes gleaming with malice. "Yes, I will use Alexander and his knowledge to further my own plans."

With a newfound sense of determination, Satan set off to uncover the truth, his mind already scheming and plotting. After all, in the game of good vs. evil, there were no rules. And Satan was determined to come out on top.

"Alexander's lifeless body lies abandoned in a dark, desolate cave, a mere vessel for his spirit that roams the present. Find him, bring him to me," Satan's voice echoed through the cavern, seeping into every crevice. His words dripped with malice and urgency, urging his followers to act swiftly and without mercy. "We will wage war on both ends of time, nothing can stop us. And to the one who brings me Alexander, I will bestow upon them the title of my second in command." A chill ran down the spines of those who heard Satan's proclamation, fear and greed swirling in their hearts.

The stakes were high, and they were willing to do whatever it took to claim the coveted position. "The location of Alexander's body is hidden within a cave that once served as David's sanctuary," Satan revealed, a sinister grin spreading across his face. "Dig through David's writings, search every nook and cranny. The reward is worth the risk, my loyal servants." The air was thick with anticipation and determination, as Satan's followers set off on their mission. The promise of power and glory fueled their every step, blinding them to the consequences of their actions. But little did they know, the true and power behind Alexander's spirit and the dangers that lie ahead.

Only time will tell who will emerge victorious in this battle of good and evil. David had meticulously recorded every detail; the location will be revealed. I carefully stashed away his writings for this moment. He will lead us to Alexander." Satan revisited the day of the crucifixion, replaying every moment with fresh eyes. And there, he noticed what had eluded him before. Simon's son, Alexander, was by his side as they made their way to Jerusalem. In slow motion, Satan watched as Alexander followed Simon into the desert. "He was there," Satan exclaimed. "Alexander witnessed Simon's crucifixion. He was the one Elijah and Michael were guarding."

Fueled by rage, Satan unleashed his demons into the fiery abyss, causing chaos in the demon hierarchy and command structure. No demon was safe from his vengeance in this moment. "Michael...I am coming for you. Do you hear me? Nothing can stop me!" bellowed Satan. With a newfound determination, he scoured through the

Scriptures and David's unpublished writings, searching for any mention of the hidden cave. Multiple locations were identified, and Satan set out to destroy them all, hoping that one of them might hold the body of Alexander. Meanwhile, he sent legions of demons to Utah on a mission to capture Alexander's spirit and eliminate anyone who stood in their way.

* * * *

Michael scoffed at the idea that Satan was unstoppable. "We have had this conversation before," Michael retorted. He summoned Elijah and Daniel and warned them of the impending battle. "You must be ready; they do not know the exact location of the cave, but they are getting closer. They see Alexander as a threat and will stop at nothing to eliminate him. We have a responsibility to ensure the safety of two individuals in two distinct worlds and time periods, separated by two millennia." Michael then summoned Gabriel, who appeared promptly. Standing before all the angels, Michael declared, "This is a battle for the sake of all humanity. We must protect Alexander and Dr. Spigelman, both descendants of Simon, the King's most revered and blessed aide. Simon endured great suffering for our Lord and King. And now, it is our duty to fulfill the Lord's promise of protection for his sons." With that, Gabriel launched an attack on the demons, inflicting heavy casualties upon Satan's armies in their search for the protected cave.

As the angels waged war, the earth itself seemed to tremble in anticipation of the outcome. Gabriel's mighty sword flashed with heavenly light, cutting through the darkness of Satan's minions. The air crackled with the clash of good and evil, each strike sending ripples of energy through the very fabric of reality. Michael, with his unwavering determination, coordinated their celestial army, ensuring the protection of Alexander and Dr. Spigelman across time and space. Meanwhile, Dr. Spigelman, a descendant of Simon, pored over ancient texts, unaware of the impending danger. His very existence was a threat to Satan's plans, and the demons were drawing closer, their malicious intent growing with each discovery.

Satan's rage only intensified as his demons returned, bearing news of their failed attempts to locate Alexander's body. "You fools!" he roared, his voice echoing through the depths of hell. "Your incompetence knows no bounds! I will not be thwarted by these pathetic mortals!" In his fury, he unleashed a torrent of fire and brimstone upon his followers, a terrifying display of his power. The screams of the damned echoed through the underworld, a stark reminder of the price of failure. Yet, even as he vented his wrath, Satan's mind worked feverishly, plotting and scheming a new strategy. He would not rest until he held the upper hand once more.

Little did they know that their efforts were in vain, as Michael, with his divine foresight, had already anticipated their every move. "Prepare for their assault," he commanded his angels. "We must stand firm and protect what is rightfully ours. The legacy of Simon of Cyrene and the truth he carries must be preserved." And so, the celestial warriors readied themselves, their eyes shining with unwavering resolve. They knew the stakes were higher than ever, and they would not falter in their duty to protect humanity from Satan's relentless wrath.

Meanwhile, Michael and his angels surrounded Alexander and Dr. Spigelman with a protective shield, rendering them invisible to Satan and his forces. In that moment, they were truly safe.

CHAPTER 30

DEBI PRAYS

Debi was well aware that she could not escape from Adam. He did not belong to the realm of the living, but rather to the dead. He was not a mere mortal, but a demonic creation of Satan himself. The truth finally dawned on her. "I never truly believed in the existence of demons, angels, God and Satan, but now it all feels so real. If only I could be spared, God," Debi prayed. On the other hand, Arie was not convinced. As he left the coffee shop, he made up his mind to head back home, pack his belongings, and leave town. He knew of a place where even Satan could not track him down, he thought. In a frenzy, he gathered his stash of money, fashionable clothes, and expensive jewelry. "I will hide until this storm passes," he declared. Arie hastily grabbed his belongings and made his way downstairs to meet his cab and head to the airport. As the cab driver loaded Arie's baggage into the trunk, a glimmering gold coin slipped out of one of the bags and rolled onto the street. Arie went to retrieve the coin, narrowly missing being hit by a speeding car. He let out a sigh of relief and glanced back at the cab driver, "Not today. It's not my time to die," he chuckled, before stepping back onto the street to retrieve the shiny coin. But fate had other plans as

Arie carelessly walked into the path of a fast-approaching delivery truck. The driver did not bother to slow down, and Arie was left lifeless on the road. The cab driver's eyes turned an eerie shade of orange as he looked at the lifeless body lying on the street. "Yes, today," he said with a sinister laugh, as he disappeared into thin air, revealing his true identity as Adam. Meanwhile, Debi had returned home and locked all the doors, but she knew that it was not enough to keep this evil at bay. She had let her guard down and had foolishly gotten involved in something beyond her understanding. Her mind drifted back to her childhood days at church camp. "I was saved," she reminisced, "but I did not truly comprehend what that meant. I was taught about Jesus and the Devil, but it all seemed like a distant concept until now." She resolved to pray.

"Dear Lord, it has been a while since I last spoke to You. I hope You remember me. I may not have done much for You or attended church regularly, but my Sunday school teacher said that You always hear our prayers. I am scared, Lord. I know You are real. I surrender myself to You and seek Your protection against Adam and Satan. Amen."

With renewed faith, Debi rose from her knees. Debi's anxiety was evident as she paced restlessly in the living room, until Adam suddenly appeared in the kitchen. "Well, well, if it isn't Debi," he greeted her with a smirk. "Did you miss me?" Debi's reaction was a mix of shock and fear, as she cried out, "What do you want?" sensing his menacing presence. "I know you don't have any information," Adam replied calmly. "I was actually on my way to end you, but I have more pressing matters to attend to. Oh, and by the way, have you seen Dr. Spigelman?" Debi quickly denied any knowledge, to which Adam warned, "Just remember, this is between you and me. You can't escape me." With that, he disappeared, leaving Debi relieved that she was temporarily spared from danger.

CHAPTER 31

THE DISCOVERY: THREE MONTHS LATER

Professor Spigelman spent the next three months preparing for a six-month excavation project, completely unaware of the ongoing battle surrounding him. Surprisingly, he had not received a single word from Alex, the mysterious voice who had revealed him salve in his office. Perhaps all Alex desired was for him to dig in this desolate and unrecorded location.

While Alexander lay in safety in his own time, it was the 21st century and Professor Spigelman now found himself standing in his new office, overlooking the very excavation site that had consumed his thoughts.

As he took in his surroundings, he couldn't help but contemplate his living quarters, a cramped eight-foot-by-sixteen-foot trailer, complete with a small desk and a restroom. In an effort to make the space more conducive to work, he had brought his own draftsman table, though it was clear that the trailer was not meant to serve as a suitable workspace. Despite the windows on either side of the trailer, allowing in light and air, it was not enough to combat the stifling heat. The small food preparation area, equipped with only a microwave and sink, was a stark reminder of just how isolated and primitive this location truly was. The constant rumble of the gasoline generator powering the trailer was nearly as loud as the nearby heavy equipment, adding to the overall sense of discomfort and unease.

As Spigelman began to settle into the trailer, he was abruptly interrupted by JoAnn, who informed him of a local newspaper reporter who wanted to interview him.

JoAnn was a twenty-one-year old student from Brigham Young University, her youthful energy and curiosity fueling her passion for ancient history and archaeology. She was chosen by Professor Spigelman to accompany him on his latest expedition, serving as his public relations liaison. Despite her lack of experience, JoAnn's enthusiasm and quick wit caught the professor's attention, but most of all she reminded him of his secretary, Pattie. As Professor Spigelman emerged from the vehicle, the desert wind howled, tossing sand and dust into his face and eyes. As the professor took a deep breath the gritty air coated his tongue.

"I'm Professor Spigelman," he introduced himself to the waiting reporter. Hi, I'm Adam, greeted the reporter, with a firm handshake. "Nice to meet you, Professor. I have a few questions for you." As the interview progressed, Adam soon realized that the professor was venturing into uncharted territory, unaware of what lay beneath the surface. "Why choose this location if it's not even on a map?" Adam probed. "Wouldn't it be wiser to dig at a known site?"

"This is the only site I could get approved," said the desperate Professor Spigelman, his voice tinged with frustration and disappointment. But Adam, the enigmatic young man with a glint in his eye, simply chuckled. "I can fix that," he said, his voice dripping with confidence. "I can have a site ready in just two days – a known ancient city waiting to reveal its secrets." The professor's eyes widened in disbelief. "You can do that?" he asked, his voice trembling with excitement. Adam's grin widened. "Of course," he said, his voice laced with mystery. "It's all done with lights and mirrors."

"I was led to dig here," Professor Spigelman insisted, his tone turning more serious. "Led?" questioned Adam, his eyebrows raised in curiosity. "Who led you?" "It's not a who," the professor replied, his voice hushed. "It's a what. It was like a spiritual calling...you know." "I'm afraid I don't know," said Adam, his tone now tinged with skepticism.

"So, you won't change your mind and dig where I know you'll find treasure, is that right?" The professor's expression turned resolute. "Yes, that's right," he said firmly. "For some reason, I must dig here." In that moment, Adam knew that Professor Spigelman was the one they had been searching for – the one with the key to unlocking the secrets of Simon of Cyrene. And what surprised him even more was that the professor seemed to have no knowledge of what he was about to uncover.

Adam's mind raced as he contemplated the possibilities of why Alexander chose Spigelman. Could it be that the professor was a descendant of Simon of Cyrene, and that is the reason Alexander had visited? And if so, how could he not know about his own lineage and the treasure that awaited him? This was just the beginning of a thrilling adventure, one that would push the boundaries of what they thought was possible and reveal secrets that had been buried for centuries. And as the wind howled and the sun began to set, Adam knew that this was only the beginning of a journey that would change both of their lives forever.

The blazing sun beat down on the excavation site, its intense rays searing through the air and onto the parched earth. It had been two long, grueling months since Professor Spigelman and his team had started their quest to uncover hidden treasures of the past. But so far, their efforts had yielded nothing but disappointment. As he trudged to the site, the professor's heart was heavy and his spirits low. But he refused to give up, determined to uncover the secrets that lay buried beneath the surface. He started up the generator, the loud hum breaking the peaceful morning silence, and poured himself a cup of hot coffee. Lost in his thoughts, he was jolted back to reality by a familiar voice echoing through the excavation site. It was Alex, the Voice, who had convinced the professor to dig in this very spot. "Professor," Alex greeted him with a mischievous grin. "Thanks for digging here." "A lot of good it has done," the professor grumbled. "Where is this life-changing discovery you promised?" "It's coming, I promise you," Alex replied cryptically. "But there are things you need to know, things I can't tell you just yet. Just remember, things are never what they seem. Look deeper." As Alex spoke, the professor couldn't help but feel a shiver run down his spine. There was something about this young man that was both intriguing and unsettling. And when he mentioned Jesus and the Bible, the professor couldn't help but feel a surge of emotions welling up inside him. Before he could ask any questions, Alex was gone, disappearing into the shadows of the excavation site. "Where did he go now?" the professor wondered aloud. "I wish he would stop doing that." But deep down, the professor knew that there was more to Alex than met the eye. And as he returned to his work, he couldn't shake off the feeling that today would be a day that would go down in history. Little did he know, the events that were about to unfold would change his life forever.

The sun was peaking over the horizon, casting a soft orange glow across the city. The streets were quiet, but for the sound of birds chirping and the distant hum of early morning traffic. The Professor sat at his desk, the light from his lamp casting a warm glow on the stacks of paperwork in front of him. He rubbed his tired eyes, feeling the weight of exhaustion settling in his bones, he had a lot on his plate, and the pressure was weighing heavily on him. He glanced at the clock, realizing with a start that the sun would be up soon. He needed to finish this paperwork before the rest of his team arrived for work. He couldn't afford to waste any time. He grabbed his pen and began to scribble furiously, the sound of it scratching against the paper echoing through the quiet room. But as he worked, his mind couldn't help but wander. What if they didn't find anything? What if this dig went cold like so many others? The thought sent a shiver down his spine. He couldn't let that happen. He couldn't let down the people counting on him. The Professor leaned back in his chair, running a hand through his hair. He could feel the weight of responsibility pressing down on him, threatening to consume him. But he couldn't give up. He wouldn't give up. He was determined to see this case through, no matter what it took. He closed his eyes and took a deep breath, trying to calm the storm of emotions raging inside him. He needed to stay focused, to keep a clear head. And he would. He would find the answers they were looking for, no matter how long it took. As the first rays of sunlight filtered through the blinds, Dr Spigelman opened his eyes and got back to work. He may be tired and overwhelmed, but he was also determined and driven. And with that, he knew he could overcome any obstacle that came his way.

THREE HOURS LATER

The day began like any other, with the warm sun slowly melting away the morning mist, revealing the promise of a typical day at the excavation site. But as the hours passed, a palpable shift in the air became evident. A sense of fear crept in, gripping everyone at the site with an icy grip. The once tranquil atmosphere now pulsated with an ominous energy, as if the very earth beneath their feet was holding its breath in anticipation of what was to come. Alex, the lead archaeologist, felt a chill run down his spine as he surveyed the site. He couldn't shake the feeling that today's discoveries would be monumental, but not in the way they had hoped. It was as if the dark forces of the universe had converged upon this very spot, ready to unleash their wrath upon the unsuspecting team. As the team continued to dig, the tension grew thicker with each passing moment. The normally confident and composed professor now had a look of fear etched on his face. He knew that whatever they uncovered today would be more than just a historical find. It would be a portal into a dark and sinister world beyond their wildest imaginations. But nothing could have prepared them for what they were about to unearth. As the sun reached its peak in the sky, the ground trembled beneath their feet, as if a beast was stirring from its slumber. And then, it happened. The earth split open, revealing a tomb unlike any they had ever seen. And from within, a dark evil emerged, engulfing everything in its path. Satan's plan to destroy the church and deceive humanity had been unleashed. And as the team looked on in horror, they realized that this was no ordinary excavation site. This was a battleground between good and evil, with their very lives at stake. And as they stood face to face with the embodiment of pure evil, they knew that this day would forever be etched in their minds as the day they uncovered the ultimate truth about the world.

The workers trudged through the dusty, rocky terrain, sweat dripping down their faces as they toiled under the hot sun. Their tools scraped against the hard earth, their voices echoing in the stillness of the desert. But this was no ordinary excavation. This was a search for something beyond value, beyond comprehension. As they dug deeper into the ground, their hearts raced with anticipation. Each shovelful of dirt brought them closer to their goal, closer to uncovering the truth that had eluded the world for centuries. And then, in a moment of sheer disbelief, it happened. A cry went up from one of the workers, a cry that was quickly echoed by the others.

They had found it. The tomb of all tombs. The one that would change everything. But as they approached the sealed entrance, an ominous feeling crept over them. The words etched into the stone were like a warning, a chilling reminder of the power that lay within. "Jesus of Nazareth" it read, as if taunting them with its implications. The foreman halted their progress, his eyes scanning the area for any signs of danger. This was no ordinary tomb, he knew. This was a tomb steeped in history, a tomb that held secrets beyond their wildest imaginations. And so they waited, the tension building with each passing moment, until finally, the arrival of Dr. Alexander Spigelman signaled the go-ahead to proceed. With the utmost respect, they cleared away the layers of dust that had settled upon the tomb, revealing the markings that would change the course of history. "Jesus of Nazareth - King of the Jews" it proclaimed, the words etched in bold letters that seemed to glow in the dim light.

And in that moment, the world stood still.

Within hours, the news spread like wildfire, capturing the attention of every nation. The body of Christ Jesus had been found, and the world was left reeling in shock and awe. For this was no ordinary discovery. This was a discovery that would shake the very foundations of faith and belief. And as the world grappled with the implications of their find, one thing was certain - nothing would ever be the same again.

Dr. Spigelman strode confidently to the podium, his sharp eyes scanning the room of eager reporters. The air was thick with anticipation as cameras flashed and pens scribbled, capturing every word that would soon be spoken. The professor's voice boomed throughout the room as he began his address. "We will leave no stone unturned and no test untested," he declared, his voice ringing with determination. "We will use the most modern DNA testing available to identify this body." The room was silent, hanging on every word. "If this is the body of Jesus, son of Mary, we will know it." His words sent shivers down Adam's spine as he stood in the front row, his eyes fixed on the professor. With each passing moment, the intensity in the room seemed to grow, as if the weight of history was resting on their shoulders. "This body is well preserved for a two-thousand-year-old corpse," Dr. Spigelman continued, "and has plenty of hair to do DNA testing." The entire room seemed to hold their breath as he spoke, the gravity of the situation sinking in. Just then, Adam spoke up, his voice cutting through the silence. "For DNA to work, you must have something to compare it to. Do you have such a comparison?" The professor's gaze turned to Adam, his expression serious. "We know that an ossuary was found in 2002 that holds the remains of James, the brother of Jesus and son of Joseph," he answered confidently. "We believe that this will be the vital key to unlock the mystery of Jesus." A murmur went through the crowd as the implications of this statement sank in. This could be the breakthrough they had all been waiting for. But as the excitement grew, so did the questions. "Do you believe that this is truly the body of Jesus, King of the Jews?" shouted a reporter. Dr. Spigelman paused, his eyes scanning the room once again before answering. "It is too early to tell," he said, "but my first impression is that the body of Jesus has been found, it appears that the disciples did steal the body of Jesus." Gasps and murmurs erupted throughout the room, as the realization of what this could mean settled in. Emotions were running high, and the anticipation was almost palpable. But just as quickly as it had begun, the press conference was brought to a close. "No more questions," JoAnn interjected, her voice firm. "Dr. Spigelman will hold another press conference when we have more information to be shared." As the reporters began to file out of the room, the professor couldn't shake the intense feeling that this discovery was only the beginning of something much larger.

Dr. Spigelman could hardly believe it. He, a mere scientist, was now the most famous person in the world. People clamored for his attention, begging for interviews and autographs. And yet, he found himself alone in his secluded hideaway, relishing in his newfound fame. As he patted himself on the back, he couldn't help but remember the warning Alex had given him the last time they spoke: "Everything is not always what it seems." With a heavy sigh, he sank into his chair and gazed out the window, lost in thought. He had always been a curious man, but now that curiosity seemed to be his downfall. He couldn't resist picking up the note that lay on the table in front of him. He hesitated, unsure if he wanted to know the truth behind it, but his curiosity got the best of him. He unfolded it and read the words written in elegant script: As Jonah was directed to preach to the city of Nineveh, so will you be directed to prove your discovery a counterfeit. Look deep to see the clue I'm leaving you. Signed: Alexander, son of Simon of Cyrene, Dr. Spigelman's heart raced as he tried to make sense of the cryptic message. What did it mean? Was someone trying to discredit his groundbreaking discovery?

Just as he was lost in thought, the phone rang, startling him back to reality. He quickly walked across the room to answer it, his mind still reeling from the mysterious note. "Hello?" he answered, trying to sound composed. "Professor, this is JoAnn. Is everything okay? I haven't heard from you all afternoon." Dr. Spigelman took a deep breath, grateful for the distraction. "Yes, I'm fine. I was just getting ready to turn in for the night. What's up?" But deep down, he couldn't shake the feeling that things were far from fine. He had a sinking feeling that his fame had come with a heavy price, one that he may not be able to pay.

"Listen, I need to remind you about tomorrow. It's going to be a whirlwind of a day, starting with a 7:00 a.m. meeting. Then you have three more lined up back-to-back. And I'll be picking you up at the ungodly hour of 6:30 in the morning. Got it?" And as he hung up the phone and sank back into his chair, he couldn't help but wonder what other secrets lay hidden in the shadows, waiting to be uncovered. Dr. Spigelman tried to push the note out of his mind as he prepared for bed, but it lingered like a menacing shadow. "What does it mean? Jonah and Nineveh? Counterfeit?" As he lay in bed, his thoughts spun like a tornado, searching for answers.

But sleep came, and with it, a dream that felt more like a nightmare. In it, he was standing at a podium, announcing his groundbreaking discovery of the "body of Christ." The room erupted in chaos, with people clamoring for answers and demanding proof. Suddenly, the scene shifted, and he saw the destruction that his discovery had caused. The world's religious institutions were crumbling, and the once faithful followers were turning against their own beliefs. Churches were being burned, and preachers were being beaten to death in the streets. The images were vivid, and Dr. Spigelman could feel his heart racing with fear and guilt. What had he unleashed upon the world?

The government's actions were beyond cruel - they were downright malicious. They ripped the nonprofit tax status from the churches, greedily demanding back payments and seizing the holy properties to sell for their own gain. The very Bible, the cornerstone of faith for millions, was deemed a dangerous work of fiction and callously rounded up in droves to be burned. And the Christians - oh, the Christians - were hunted and persecuted, forced into hiding as their faith was deemed a threat to the rulers' power. It was a dark, dystopian world where the government had the audacity to require all job applicants and welfare recipients to publicly denounce Jesus before granting assistance. Can you even imagine the horror? As the professor bore witness to this evil, he couldn't help but realize that it was all happening because of his own discovery. He had caught a glimpse of a world without boundaries, where the devil himself reigned supreme. The Antichrist had been unleashed and there was no turning back. His mind was in turmoil, and he couldn't shake off the haunting visions. But as he drifted back into a restless sleep, one thing was certain, tomorrow was not going to be an ordinary day.

Suddenly, he jolted upright in bed, drenched in a cold sweat as his alarm blared. His heart raced as he looked around, holding his breath until he realized it was all just a dream. Just a nightmare, but what a nightmare it was, not real at all. The disaster he had just witness was a bad dream that had not come to pass yet. But the fear lingered, haunting him as he went about his day, constantly reminding himself, "It was just a dream." As Professor Spiegelman gets ready to bask in the spotlight of his newfound fame, he could not shake the feeling of fear.

As God had warned Lot not to look back at the destruction of Sodom and Gomorrah, He is now warning you of the impending doom of Satan's deceit. Nothing is ever as it seems on the surface - you must look deeper. And in this perilous world, where the lines between good and evil are blurred, it's more important than ever to trust in the Word and never let your guard down. For the Devil is always lurking, ready to pounce on those who are not vigilant. Remember, everything has a deeper meaning - don't be fooled by the Devil's lies. Jesus is alive and He there for you.

THE END

He's Alive!!!

Mary ran to the tomb of Jesus her Lord; her soul was heavy for He was with her no more;

With spices in hand her respect she was there to apply, the stone would be heavy but she must go and try;

The tomb was opened the stone rolled away, the world changed forever as she paused that day to pray;

The dark and gloomy tomb reserved for the dead, gleamed brightly around her as she ducked in her head;

The first thing she saw was an angel glowing bright, Sitting on the slab and she was filled with fright;

Who are you looking for here among the dead? The Master has arisen don't you remember what He said?

Death could not hold the perfect lamb of life; the tomb gave Him up to be your eternal sacrifice;

He who was sinless became sin for you and I, He who was perfect was now sentenced to die;

Like a lamb, Jesus was led to the cross for slaughter, Never making a sound His blood was placed on the alter;

Look no more among the dead, the angel said; look instead to the clouds and see the crown that sits on His head;

He has risen to the throne at the right hand of the Father, to sit in judgment of those who said faith was too much of a bother;

Satan could not stop Jesus' mission to the cross, the rest is up to us to accept or be counted a loss;

Praise God, Praise God, He died for me, Praise God, Praise God, He lives for all.. ...don't you see.

© BS Poteat

www.ingramcontent.com/pod-product-compliance
Lightning Source LLC
LaVergne TN
LVHW041708070526
838199LV00045B/1253